SAINTS AND SINNERS:
the folk of Mystic Evermore

Written by

Cecelia Hopkins-Drewer

ASIN: B07D1FPG4Y
ISBN: 978-0-6481160-4-2 (6x9 paperback)

Published by CGH Literacy Institute,
Adelaide, South Australia, 2018.

CONTENTS

From **The Raven** by Edgar Allan Poe
Foreword: There is None Perfect

FROM *THE RAVEN*
BY EDGAR ALLAN POE

"…But the Raven still beguiling all my fancy into smiling,
Straight I wheeled a cushioned seat in front of bird, and bust and
door;
Then, upon the velvet sinking, I betook myself to linking
Fancy unto fancy, thinking what this ominous bird of yore—
What this grim, ungainly, ghastly, gaunt, and ominous bird of yore
Meant in croaking 'Nevermore'."

Verse: 12

FOREWORD: THERE IS NONE PERFECT

"Someone said 'we had all sinned' - I think it might have been the minister at the Episcopalian church I visited once, even though I think I'm more of a philosophical Buddhist. As I look around I see, none of my friends are actually perfect, but I love every one of them. I am inclined to think, that whatever happens, there is some sort of plan for everybody."

(Bridget Etheridge's Journal)

So where is this all leading?

PARABLE FOUR: BETRAYED BY LOVE

I don't think Christy Strahan was a slut. I think, on the contrary, she was a good girl and loyal friend. She noticed Eduard Nevermore as soon as he returned to town, but he displayed an obvious preference for Lena Lenore. Christy made no move to interfere in Eduard and Lena's relationship, and did not reveal her true feelings for Eduard until he indicated readiness to date other girls.

(Bridget Etheridge's journal)

Although their house was near the centre of Mystic Evermore, the Strahan family had somehow escaped being marked by the peculiarities of the area. Grandma Strahan ran the general-store-combined-pharmacy in the shopping mall. She knew all the gossip about who was related, and who was courting in Mystic Evermore. What Grandma did not know for sure, she probably made up, and Grandma had an acceptable explanation for everything.

Robbie Strahan was a plumber and had seen everything there was to see in the underside of people's houses. He was a simple man, who dressed as a tradesman in navy overalls and tied a red bandana around his neck. When he entered a smelly zone, such as a sewer, the bandana doubled as a makeshift facemask.

His wife Barb Strahan was the perfect mother, who wore skirts, stayed home to look after the children and served on parents' committees. When business was busy, Barb helped Grandma out in the Strahan General Store; and now that the children were grown, she was often to be found working in the store.

Eighteen year old Christy Strahan was their first daughter and a senior at Mystic Evermore High. She tied her hair into a casual knot on the back of her head and decorated it with bright ribbons. Christy strived to look exotic, as all the Strahan's were blessed with dark good looks. She was sporty and popular with the boys, although she generally did not date, and appeared to be waiting for someone special. That was until the orphaned Eduard Nevermore came to town to stay with his uncle Sebastian.

Sixteen year old Zarah Strahan was a junior at Mystic Evermore High. The two sisters were very much alike, although Zarah was generally lighter and finer boned than Christy. Zarah shared her classes with other teens like Jamie Lenore, Jeroma Tilton, Netta Davis and Paul Booth.

Benji Strahan was their younger brother. He had straight hair he kept cropped very short, and he was good at math and science. So good in fact, that he joined Zarah's class for some lessons. He wasn't a genius at English however, so he was still officially a year below Zarah, and two years below Christy at Mystic Evermore High.

Zarah was hurrying home from school Friday afternoon because she had promised to help Grandma in the store. It was really Christy's job, but the older sister was always out with Eduard Nevermore nowadays.

Christ had been disappointed when Eduard appeared more attracted to the tragic Lena Lenore, who had lost her parents in an accident.Eduard and Lena had dated for some weeks, but appeared to break-up during the holidays. Subsequently, Eduard noticed Christy was still interested in him. The young couple celebrated their one month anniversary just after Labour Day.

Zarah didn't really mind, taking over Christy's shifts. Because she adored helping Grandma in the store. Anyway, Christy would be expected to do her bit while Zarah was busy performing in the Mystic Evermore High Musical extravaganza around Columbus Day.

She reached the house and unlocked the door, then she padded to her bedroom and took off her school uniform, throwing it down on her bed. A few minutes later she was neatly attired in the shirt and slacks grandma insisted she wear for work in the store. The shirt had "Strahan's" embroidered over the breast pocket and the slacks were modest for bending down to stock the shelves.

The Strahan house and store were located close together, so Zarah simply walked across to the store. The bell tinkled merrily as she opened the glass door and entered.

"Hello, Grandma," Zarah cried, approaching the checkout.

"There's my girl, Zarah," Grandma Strahan replied. "Now that you are here, I would like to take my coffee break and rest my feet for five minutes. Could you manage the till?"

"Sure, Grandma," Zarah said, and took her place behind the till.

Grandmother was looking a little tired, Zarah observed. The old woman worked long hours, and although a small town like Mystic Evermore did not really require late night shopping, Grandma insisted they provide extended hours on Thursday and Friday evenings. The store was even open two hours on Sunday afternoon.

Barbara Strahan nodded to her daughter from behind the pharmacists' counter. The pharmacy was Zarah's favourite part of the store, because it was full of soaps and perfumes as well as medicines.

Both her Mother and Grandmother had their pharmacist certificates and if neither of them was in the store the counter had to close. Zarah was allowed to sell the occasional soap or perfume, but she could not dispense medicine.

The shop bell rang and some of her school classmates passed through with their parents on the way home from school. Jeroma Tilton bought a lipstick, while her mother Lilibet collected a basket of groceries. The older brother, Javier, who always insisted his name was pronounced with a "J" was a distinctive figure in his long black coat.

Lena Lenore passed through the store with her cousin Jamie. Zarah was busy serving a customer, but out of the corner of her eye, she saw Lena and Javier exchange gazes. Then Lena crossed the floor to check Javier's score on the gaming machine Grandma had insisted on installing so the youth 'had something to do'.

Everyone knew that Lena and Javier were 'good friends'. At one stage, it had looked as though Javier was planning to ask Lena out, but Zarah figured he had a roving eye and had not settled down to one girl yet.

Fenton Etheridge passed by with Carlice Favor. Those two still hung out together constantly, although their relationship appeared to have cooled since Fenton's Mother had been killed. Grief was a great romance dampener.

"Thank you Zarah," Grandma Strahan said, appearing out of the back room. "I can take the till again if you like. There is a lot of unpacking to do in the store room."

"Alright Grandma," Zarah said. She finished serving her current customer and slid out from behind the counter. Grandmother cleverly slid into place and faced the next customer. It was a routine perfected from years of practise.

Zarah walked to the rear of the store and through the door marked 'Staff Only'. Unpacking the crates was hard work, but it was also something she loved doing. Every day was like Christmas, with so many deliveries!

There was fresh food to ticket and place on the shelves, glossy magazines to unwrap out of their plastic coverings and place on the magazine rack; boxes of newly printed books for the small book-stand, and all kinds of fascinating products that the Strahan General Store sold.

Around five-thirty pm, Mother clocked off and returned to their home to prepare the family meal. Zarah remained in the back room unpacking. As customer numbers slowed in the store around six, she began to re-stock the shop floor with new items she had loaded onto the push trolley. This allowed her to keep Grandmother company and the two chatted as they worked.

"How is your sister?" Grandmother asked, as they worked side-by-side to fill the shelves. "I hardly ever see her anymore."

"She is always with Eduard Nevermore," Zarah said. "He appears very protective of her and they seem very happy."

"His grandfather was a nice young man," Grandma Strahan remarked. "Very pleasant, and very well mannered. He knew how to show a girl a nice time on a date."

"Why did you break up?" Zarah asked curiously.

"I wanted to settle down get married," Grandma Strahan said. "And I could tell Edward Nevermore wanted to travel and see the world. So I didn't let things get too serious... if you know what I mean..."

"I think so," Zarah murmured. She actually had no experience of boys yet.

"And then when I saw your grandfather looking at me... I thought that's the boy for me!" Grandmother continued. "So I told Edward we should take a little break."

" That spring, Edward and his brother Darren left Mystic Evermore," Grandma continued. "I only heard from them once or twice. After a few weeks had passed, I thought it was alright to give your grandfather a nice smile or two."

"Grandma, you were a naughty girl," Zarah exclaimed.

"I like to think of it as smart," Grandmother Strahan said. "And I would like to think both my granddaughters were as smart as I am."

"I'm probably not," Zarah said with a sigh. She liked to talk to her father's apprentice Wilson Booth after he knocked off work, and although Wilson appeared to enjoy talking to her as well, he gave no sign of looking at her the same way she looked at him. "You know how I feel about Wilson."

"He is a nice young man," Grandmother said. "I am glad your father gave him a chance."

Wilson Booth's father was a distant cousin of Great-Grandma Booth, who was an even greater legend around town than even Grandma Strahan. Maybe because they were black, or perhaps because of the rumours that had always surrounded the Booth family, Wilson had been harassed at school.

He had been harassed to the point of dropping out, and had been on the verge of turning bad, when Robbie Strahan offered to take him on as an apprentice. As far as Zarah could see, the arrangement appeared to be working well.

Her father, Robbie Strahan was a tradesperson, and did not have a snobby or racist bone in his body. Moreover, his business piped other people's excrement away from their houses and taught him all people were alike when it came to producing waste.

The pioneer families could all pretend to be better than the rest of the town, and run their fancy Agrarian Council, but Robbie knew that they flushed their toilets the same as everybody else. Perhaps even a little more often because they could afford to!

Under Robbie's watchful eye, Wilson was becoming a skilled plumber who was able to contribute positively to the plumbing business. He would one day either take over Robbie's business or open one of his own.

Wilson's younger brother Paul was around Zarah's age and also struggling to stay in school. Robbie was considering taking Paul on as a second apprentice after his seventeenth birthday.

"Like I said," Zarah continued. "Christy seems very happy with Eduard Nevermore. Except when she gets to worrying that he wants to be back with his former girlfriend, Lena."

"I'm sure she has nothing to worry about," Grandma Strahan said wisely. "I heard a little rumour about Lena Lenore."

"What was that?" Zarah asked curiously. Grandmother did have a knack for getting all the gossip out of people.

"Miss Lenore may have had a little fling with Damien Nevermore," Grandma Strahan suggested. "I don't think that is something a nice boy like Eduard would get over quickly."

Zarah laughed. "You are wicked, Grandmother," she said. "Wasn't Damien Nevermore going out with Didge?'

"This was before Bridget Etheridge came to town," Grandmother Strahan remarked.

"If it is true, Eduard appears to have forgiven Lena," Zarah remarked. "They all seem to be good friends."

"Eduard may well have forgiven Lena, but a young man would never feel quite the same about a girl again after that, let me tell you," Grandma Strahan declared. "Eduard will have decided that your sister Christy, who is sweet and faithful to him is the better choice as his girlfriend."

"Yes," Zarah said. "I agree, Christy has nothing to worry about. But you know Christy, she does worry."

"A young lady has to have confidence in herself," Grandmother observed. "Or else, you never know what could go wrong."

"Oh yes," Zarah said. "I try to have confidence too. It's just, I don't think Wilson sees me as a girlfriend."

"It is very clever of you to recognise the fact," Grandmother Strahan said. "There will be boys who do want you as a girlfriend."

"I expect so," Zarah said. Sometimes it was just easier to agree with her Grandmother. She turned the empty trolley towards the store room door. "I will put this away."

"You do that dear, and then it will be time for us to go home," Grandma Strahan said. The older woman walked to the glass doors at the front of the store and locked them securely. Then she turned to tidying some of the displays.

Zarah pushed the trolley towards the back of the shop and out the door into the store room. It was dark in there, so she stopped to turn on the light. As she did so, she seemed to hear a slight sound.

The noise was a scuffling or a shuffling.

Zarah opened the cupboard door and a large rat crawled out. It seemed bigger than a normal rat and it had two long teeth projecting to each side of its mouth. She screamed.

"What is it dear?" her Grandmother exclaimed, bustling through the door. Seeing the rat, Grandmother Strahan grabbed a broom handle. She efficiently stunned the creature and dropped it into the metal trash can. "Just a rat dear."

"It had big teeth," Zarah gasped.

"Some of them do dear," Grandmother Strahan observed equitably. "Next thing you will be telling me you think it is a vampire rat."

"A vampire rat?" Zarah exclaimed. "I have never heard of such a thing."

"There are a few funny things around Mystic Evermore, dear," Grandma said. "Your father could tell some tales as to what he's found in the sewers. I take as little notice as possible and that's how I stay safe around here. I taught your mother the same thing."

"Funny I have never seen one before," Zarah said, "In all my years as a child here!"

"Something must have stirred it up," Grandma Strahan said. "Now you make a call on your mobile phone, and you get your father to pick us up from here and take us home even though it's so close, will you?"

"Sure," Zarah said and pulled out her mobile phone. She quickly placed a call to her father, who would be finished his plumbing jobs by now even if he had worked slightly late. "Dad can you drop by the store and pick me and Gran up? Yeah thanks. We saw a giant rat with pointy teeth. Tell you about it later."

On the edge of her peripheral vision, Zarah saw her Grandmother do a strange thing. The old lady removed a wooden garden stake from a plant that was for sale, and approached the metal garbage can. Lifting the lid, she stabbed into the can viciously several times with the stake. Zarah closed her phone and walked up softly behind her grandmother. There was no longer a rat in the bin, just a pile of dust and some slimy sludge.

"Whatever did you do Grandmother?" Zarah exclaimed.

"Just a little trick Edward Nevermore taught me to keep myself safe," Grandma Strahan said. "I passed it on to your mother and father too. I guess it's your time to learn, dear. It works on anything with those pointy teeth. Or else they keep getting up again."

"It works on vampire rats?" Zarah exclaimed.

"There you go again," Grandma Strahan said. "There are no such things as vampires. Just a few funny animals with pointy teeth. Whoever told you about vampires?"

"You did!" Zarah exclaimed, but Grandmother looked blank and maintained her innocence. Zarah reflected that her grandmother must be getting vague in her old age.

Robbie arrived just then and bundled Zarah and Grandmother into his van. He did not look surprised at Zarah's description of the rat. He reported that he had seen one or two in the town sewers of late, and expected they must be getting out into the town buildings.

When Zarah asked her father what he did when he saw a giant rat, her father described stabbing it with a piece of sharpened wood, just as Grandmother had done. Indeed, he kept some sharpened wood pieces amongst his tools on purpose. It wasn't something you would really notice as a plumber has a lot of tools.

At home, the Strahan family enjoyed a delicious tea. Barb Strahan had prepared a chicken dish with just a hint of curry and butter. It was one of Zarah's favourites. Then Zarah sat down to do her homework to get it out of the way before the weekend commenced. She envied her brother Benji, who finished his mathematics within a few minutes and completed his science just as easily. His English took a bit longer, but he was working at an easier level in his humanity subjects anyway. It would be nice to be half a genius!

Christy was still out with Eduard. On date nights, she usually had dinner at a restaurant with her beau, or ate at Nevermore Manor. The Strahan parents didn't appear to worry too much about their daughter as she was always able to describe the meal she had eaten or the movie she had seen while out with Eduard. Sometimes Christy reported being on a double date with Damien and Bridget or other members of the senior class.

Their parents found these accounts very reassuring and accepted them as evidence that Christy and Eduard were being careful. As Grandmother said, Eduard Nevermore seemed like a very nice young man, and much like his Grandfather.

****

Zarah was sleeping comfortably in her bed when she was awoken by a tapping at her window. Rubbing the sleep out of her eyes, she discovered that her sister was reaching upwards using a light tree branch and calling softly to her from the ground below.

"Please let me in, Zarah," Christy whispered. "I'm a little too late tonight and Mother has locked the door. She probably assumed I had come in quietly around curfew, like I promised."

"You better hope that is what Mother assumed," Zarah hissed.

Their parents had been amazingly generous and given Christy a curfew of eleven-thirty, whereas Zarah's own curfew was more like ten on the rare nights she went out. It had something to do with Eduard Nevermore's earnest expression, soldier-like posture and solemn promise to always drive their sister home safely.

Zarah padded down to the kitchen and let her sister in through the laundry door, where they were well away from any of the bedrooms.

"Thanks, Zarah," Christy said. The teenager was teetering on her feet, barely able to stand.

Zarah took a sniff. She wasn't quite sure because she didn't drink alcohol yet herself, but: "Have you been drinking?" she asked.

"Yes," Christy said, "Damien wasn't home to stop us for once, and Eduard got the scotch out".

"Eduard isn't old enough to drink either," Zarah remarked disapprovingly.

"Eduard says he is," Christy said. "He says he's actually repeating senior year because it's so different here than where he did his senior year last time. Please don't tell anyone, it's a great secret!"

"Well even if he is older than you, and repeating senior year for some reason, he should know better than to give alcohol to you," Zarah said sharply.

"Don't be such a prissy," Christy retorted. "He just gave me some to try. Everyone tries alcohol before their twenty-first birthday you know."

"No I don't," Zarah said. "No one in my class has tried it yet, that I know of... only Paul Booth, who sipped a little of Wilson's when Wilson was running wild. Paul said it was foul - and even Wilson doesn't drink anymore, now he works for Dad."

"That's cheap stuff like beer," Christy said. "Quality scotch is different."

"I dare say," Zarah remarked sharply. "Stronger and more expensive. How much have you had?"

"Just a little Eduard gave me, and a glass I sneaked when he wasn't looking," Christy said. "It was so warming. And it put me in the mood for things I can't talk about to a little girl like you."

"I do know the facts of life," Zarah replied resentfully.

"In theory, but not in practice," Christy said. "Love is so wonderful, little sister."

"I hope you aren't doing anything that could get you pregnant," Zarah cautioned.

"Eduard says I won't get pregnant," Christy said.

"I think that's something all boys say," Zarah observed wryly.

"Like you would know anything about what boys say," Christy sneered scornfully.

"There is no need to be rude," Zarah said. "I did come down and let you inside without waking Mum and Dad."

"I'm sorry," Christy said. "I do owe you one. Truth is, I don't care if I get pregnant. I wish I would. Then Eduard would have to forget all about Lena and marry me."

"You are insecure and you are allowing it to make you run wild," Zarah observed. "From what I have heard, Eduard really cares about you."

"Then why does he always go running to comfort Lena whenever she gets depressed?" Christy said. "Any time she is feeling down, they have these deep-and-meaningfuls."

"That's sympathy," Zarah said. "What Eduard feels for you is so much better than sympathy. You ask him."

"I'm not brave enough," Christy said.

"It's no good going out with the guy if you are afraid to talk to him," Zarah observed. "And Grandmother did say Lena might have done something Eduard would not forgive."

"Hmm, what might that be?" Christy asked curiously.

"According to Grandmother, Lena may have had a slight romance with Damien Nevermore," Zarah replied.

"Nah, surely not," Christy remarked. "There's Bridget. Although, I'm not sure Didge and Damien are still together. Damien seems to hang out more with Captain Etheridge than his daughter."

"You can't mess with two brothers," Zarah observed. "It's one of those truths that uphold the universe."

"Look who's talking!" Christy sneered. "You do know Paul Booth likes you don't you? He just won't ask you out because you are too busy crushing on Wilson. Wilson is too old for you anyway, and he's seen way too much of the dark side of life."

"Paul Booth?" Zarah cried. "He's in my class and we are just good friends."

"Think about it," Christy said. She yawned. "Anyway, I need to get some sleep. Thanks again for letting me in."

Christy padded upstairs to her bedroom and Zarah followed slowly on soft slipper clad feet. Neither girl woke their parents or brother.

In the morning, Christy stayed in bed sick. Zarah was going to give her older sister a hard time about being hung over, but Christy was also sneezing and clearly had caught a cold.

Zarah had promised Grandmother Strahan that she would help out at the store in the morning. Saturday morning was a popular shopping time for people who worked during the week and the little coffee and cake unit in the center of the store was also popular with those who liked a sweet treat while out.

Zarah was almost run off her feet serving coffees and slices of cake, while Grandmother ran the till. Barbara Strahan ran the pharmacy counter dispensing medicines between ten and twelve am, before knocking off and going back to their house.

The Strahan General Store closed its glass doors at twelve thirty. Grandmother was busy counting money when Wilson Booth arrived to look at the back sink and pick up a few supplies for Zarah's father.

Grandmother suggested that Zarah help Wilson out the back, so she led the way through to the sink in the staff area behind the dispensary. "Here's the drain."

"I think it's just blocked," Wilson observed and got some tools out. He set to work, unscrewing the joined piece, washing the pipe out and screwing it back on again. "Simple really."

"Father tells me you have seen some giant rats down in the sewers," Zarah remarked. "We had one up here yesterday."

"Yes," Wilson agreed. "Your father showed me what to do to them."

"Spike them with a stick?" Zarah inquired.

"Yeah," Wilson confirmed.

"Are there a lot of them down in the pipes?" Zarah asked.

"A few," Wilson said. "But not more than your father and I can handle. We would be poor plumbers if we were afraid of a few rats."

"They are not natural are they?" Zarah observed.

"No, I would say not. One we did not stake kept coming back to life, even though it had been beaten up thoroughly," Wilson concurred. "Everyday rats are smaller, and they die easier. In traps, with a sharp blow, using baits, or even eaten by cats."

"Do you think we should tell Sherriff Favor?" Zarah asked.

Wilson appeared to think for a moment or two. Then he shook his head. "No," he said. "In this town, there's them and us."

"What do you mean?" Zarah asked. "Most towns have socio-economic variations."

"Mystic Evermore is worse than some towns," Wilson observed. "Your Dad and your Nan know how to make money, and your Dad has shown me how to make money, but we will never be part of 'them'. Them's are born with money, and they do not have to demean themselves to get it."

"Gran enjoys running the shop," Zarah objected.

"I also enjoy working for your father," Wilson said. "But I crawl under people's houses to make money. It doesn't bother me, and it doesn't bother your Dad, but it keeps us from being 'them'. No matter how much money we make."

"I see," Zarah nodded.

"These rats are coming from under houses," Wilson observed. "I would say they are 'us' business, not 'them' business. If it got to be more than rats, say cats and dogs - that might be Sheriff business."

"Wilson, can I ask you something personal?" Zarah murmured. She had been thinking about the advice she gave Christy the previous night. It was no good liking someone if you were afraid to be honest with them. Perhaps she ought to follow her own advice.

"Sure," Wilson said.

"We are good friends, aren't we?" Zarah inquired.

Wilson sighed. He looked like he suspected what was coming, and no young man really enjoys a 'deep-and-meaningful' relationship conversation with a young lady, especially one in whom he was not interested.

"We are good friends, ain't nothing gunna change that," the Apprentice declared.

"Have you ever thought about me in a girlfriend sort-of way?" Zarah asked.

"I owe your father too much to lay hands on his daughters in a disrespectful fashion," Wilson replied. "Your Dad really saved me and he has set me up. One time, before Christy started going out with Eduard, I did fancy her a little. That's the truth Zarah, but I never thought of you that way, no."

"I see," Zarah said. She had suspected as much. Christy always appealed to the boys.

"It's not my place to say," Wilson continued. "But you're at school with my brother Paul, and I think he might look at you more that way. He's smarter than me too and he's never been in any serious trouble. Not like me… don't tell him I said so though. You gotta work these things out for yourselves."

"Thanks Wilson," Zarah said. She was hurting a little, but it was better to know for sure and prepare herself to move on. "I'm curious about something else, whereabouts in your 'them' and us scenario do you place the Nevermores?"

"The Nevermores are neither to be honest," Wilson deduced. "They got money, and they helped set the town up, but Nevermore - it's a sort of odd name. They've been booted off the Agrarian Council too. They stand out, but they don't really fit in. I think your sister might be better off with me, even though I'm saying it myself."

"I think so too," Zarah said sincerely. From what she had seen last night, Christy's relationship with Eduard wasn't doing her a lot of good.

"The sink's all done," Wilson announced. "Where are these boxes for your father?"

"Over here," Zarah showed Wilson the plumbing supplies her father had ordered through the general store.

As he packed the boxes into the work van, the young man appeared to have an idea: "Say, Zarah, do you have any plans for this afternoon?"

"Not really," Zarah admitted. She always finished helping grandmother in the store before making her own plans. If Christy was well enough when she woke up again, her sister would probably go out with Eduard for a drive or something. The couple never invited Zarah to join, it was more evidence of Christy's jealous nature she could not have even her young sister around.

That meant Zarah would read a book, watch TV, play some game with Benji or call up Ivy Pinkerton. Ivy was Christy's friend really, but with Christy so busy, the older girl had started to socialize with Zarah after she had finished her church stuff on the weekends.

"Well, I promised to take Paul fishing along the Old Mill Stream, and I wondered whether you and Benji would like to come along," Wilson suggested.

Zarah thought for a moment. "I reckon Benji would like that," she said. "I might feel a bit weird with all you being boys, but as one is my brother - I'll check with him and see."

"I'll come by about two o'clock to pick you's up if you decide to come along," Wilson said.

"Sounds good," Zarah said. "But hang on, isn't the Old Mill Farm tenanted now, so local kids can't go there and play ghost anymore?"

"It is," Wilson admitted. "I hooked up the plumbing for the lady that's got it now. Right fancy piece she is too, I don't reckon she is no farmer. Maybe an artist, I think I saw an easel propped against the wall. She talks sort of old fashioned too, or maybe she's from England. Anyway, she said I could fish along there, as long as I stuck to the stream."

"Okay," Zarah said, greatly cheered. The invitation was comforting following the bad news Wilson wasn't interested in her as a girl, and indeed had been carrying a torch for her sister Christy.

"I'll see you soon." Wilson waved and drove off cheerily in the van.

Zarah helped grandmother lock up the shop. The local businesses closed Saturday afternoon, and even Grandmother took her leisure.

The day was bright and sunny as they walked the few yards back to the Strahan residence, where Barb had a fresh salad and baked pasta ready for lunch.

"Benji," Zarah said to her brother as they sat down to the meal, "Wilson has invited us fishing this afternoon if you are interested."

Benji looked pleased. Taking half his classes with the Sophomore class and half with Zarah's Junior class left him in a social no-man's land. He got along well enough with Jamie Lenore, Paul Booth and Nathan Vaughn amongst the boys, but he wasn't quite as sporty as those guys, and fitting in remained a challenge. His best friend had once been Kier Favor, but the Sheriff's son had left town when his parent's divorced.

"That sounds great," he said. "Could we go Dad?"

Robbie Strahan considered. "If Wilson's in charge it should be okay, but keep an eye out for your sister," he said. "I don't want you boys forgetting she's along and dragging her over too much rough territory."

"Yes Dad," Benji promised.

"I believe we are fishing quite locally," Zarah assured her father, although she strategically omitted any mention of the Old Mill Farm. Many of the grown-ups had been relieved when the Farm had been tenanted and the local youth no longer adventured over there.

"Have a good afternoon," Barb said. "I'm going over to Grandma's place with her for the afternoon." Grandmother Strahan often stayed over with her son and daughter-in-law, but she did have a small unit of her own with a vegetable patch and flower garden that she tended on weekends.

Christy as usual had plans with Eduard, who roared up in his red vintage car soon after lunch. The couple said they were going to visit Mount Mystic for the afternoon and do some sightseeing.

Zarah suspected they would end up parked somewhere making out, if not going straight back to the Nevermore Manor. She could see the desperation in her sister's eyes.

Although part of Zarah had always envied Christy her popularity, it was also sad that Christy could think of no other way of holding her boyfriend, than wasting an afternoon on hot and heavy petting.

Around two o'clock, Wilson drove up in his old car. Dad probably would not have minded him driving the van, but Wilson was scrupulous in sticking to using the van for plumbing work and his own old bomb for personal excursions.

Paul was seated beside his brother in the front seat, so Zarah and Benji climbed in the back. They set off for the outskirts of town and soon reached the Old Mill Farm, where Wilson pulled the car off the road and parked out of sight amongst the trees. Wilson untied the fishing rods from the roof-rack, while Paul pulled the bait bucket out of the luggage compartment.

Zarah flinched to see some of the worms were still moving, but Benji volunteered to carry the bait bucket and appeared completely undisturbed by its contents.

Zarah ended up carrying a much more tasteful package of sandwiches, Wilson had the drinks because they were heavier, and Paul had all the other bits and pieces.

They followed a route along the river, so as to encroach on the Old Mill Farm as little as possible, and avoid disturbing its inhabitant. Wilson selected a shady spot beside a wider stretch of river, where the water also looked deep. He sat down and showed Benji how to bait a hook.

"The rest is a matter of patience," the older boy said, "Although reeling the fish in does require some skill."

Wilson and Benji seemed perfectly happy sitting dangling rods in the water and half falling asleep. After seeing the worms, however, Zarah could not bear to touch the fishing equipment. She casually gazed around the area and fell into a daydream. After a while she realized Paul Booth had come to sit alongside her.

Zarah looked up at him shyly and then dropped her eyes. After weeks of crushing on Wilson, she could not get used to the idea it was Paul who liked her. If that was even true. Her sister and his brother both said so, but they might have it all wrong.

"It's just me," Paul whispered, "Paul from school."

Zarah ventured a peek. His black eyelashes were thick, and his brown eyes had a nice twinkle. His hair was cut shorter than Wilson's, as Wilson favored the style sometimes referred to as an 'afro' and Paul preferred a simple clipper cut. Paul also had a nice open face. Both boys were strong and fit, and if Wilson was a little taller, well that was because he was two years older than his brother.

"I know," Zarah murmured, "But we've never..."

"Been anywhere together?" Paul concluded. "You've hung out with Wilson at the shop."

"Yeah that was different," Zarah said. "I spend a lot of time at the shop."

"Benji seems to be enjoying fishing," Paul observed.

"Yes," Zarah agreed. It was rare to see her brother so happy away from his computer.

"Wilson said we were to stay along the river," Paul whispered, "But I would like to take a look at the farm if we don't get caught."

"So would I," Zarah said, her self-consciousness completely overcome by curiosity. "So let's sneak off."

Paul and Zarah retraced their steps along the river bank while they were under Wilson's watchful eyes, and then they crawled into some bushes from where they could peer out and survey the Old Mill Farm. All was still and quiet.

"Nobody home," Paul said.

"I'm not so sure," Zarah said.

"Did you ever really believe it was haunted?" Paul whispered.

"I don't know," Zarah said. "It was a wonderful story. The farmer's wife, who waited for her husband to return from the civil war, even after she had died from fever herself."

"Shh," Paul hissed. "I think I saw something." The sun had gone behind the clouds, and the trees shaded the farmyard, so a sort of twilight had formed. "There, the door to the mill silo is opening."

"It's the lady, whatever is she doing in there?" Zarah whispered. Sure enough the figure of a woman emerged from the old silo. Her cloak and gown were styled long, almost to the ground. Her hair and face were covered by a black scarf which must have been difficult to see through, and she wore thick leather gloves.

"What's she doing?" Paul asked. "She has something with her, down by her feet."

Zarah gave a start. "It's a giant rat", she whispered. "Gran and I found one in the store room. Wilson and Dad find them in the sewers at times too."

"There are more rats," Paul whispered. "Whatever is she doing?" "She is petting them or feeding them, maybe she even breeds them," Zarah observed.

"Do they look like they would make good pets to you?" Paul asked.

"No," Zarah whispered. "If the lady is not careful, she could lose a finger."

"I don't think so," Paul observed. "They seem to obey her."

"I'm scared," Zarah whispered. "We need to get out of here."

The teenagers backed carefully through the bushes down to the river bed once again, where they both heaved a sigh of relief. If the lady had given permission for Wilson to use the river, she would not be too angry at discovering them in its path. However, they were not exposed and they made it back safely to where Wilson and Benji sat fishing.

Wilson and Benji reluctantly agreed to pack up and return to the car. As they drove home, the sun sank below the horizon while pink and orange covered the sky, slowly dimming into black. Zarah shivered, she was glad they had not stayed out along the river any later, despite Wilson's wise provision of a flashlight.

"Thanks for taking me fishing," Benji said as Wilson dropped them off. "I had a great time."

"Me too Wilson," Zarah exclaimed. She looked at Paul. Neither of them had told the others what they had seen. "We will talk later." She scribbled her mobile number onto a scrap of paper out of her pocket and handed it to him. "Text me."

"Sure," Paul agreed. His eyes were dark and meaningful.

Zarah blushed and Benji whistled. "It's not what you think," she asserted fiercely.

"None of our business if it was," Wilson said stoically. "That right young Ben?"

"Okay, okay Sis," Benji said. "Come inside, Mum will be sure to have some tea for us."

"Lucky things," Paul said.

Wilson nodded. "We only have our father and he is not very well."

"I'm sorry to hear that," Zarah said. She vaguely thought she had heard the Wilson's father had a bad heart or something. "See you another time."

Benji and Zarah continued inside, then Wilson and Paul drove away.

****

That Saturday night had been designated as a dance evening at Mystic Evermore High School. The dance was in honor of the annual apple picking, which had already commenced with the 'gala' and 'red delicious' varieties on the farms outside town.

Zarah had bought a dress, because she had secretly been hoping to ask Wilson. However, her crush on Wilson was now officially over, and after showering to wash away the dust of the fishing expedition, she sat on her bed looking at the dress.

It was black and figure hugging, with a sprinkle of golden stars. The neck was a little low and Zarah had purchased a new push-up-bra to go under it. It would be nice to see a boy look at her the way boys always looked at Christy.

The mobile phone on her bed-side table beeped and she picked it up. It was a text from Paul. "Can you talk?" It said.

"Yeah," Zarah texted back. "Wasn't that lady weird?"

"OMG Yes," Paul texted. "Should we tell someone?"

"I dunno," Zara texted. "You going to the school dance tonight? I could see you there, as a friend."

"Okay," Paul texted. "See you there!"

Zarah continued getting dressed, but this time her efforts had purpose. She didn't usually wear make-up, but she ran into her sister's room and begged to borrowed some lipstick and blush. Zarah also let her hair hang down loose. She had to admit she looked a bit different than her usual uniformed self.

Her mobile phone beeped again. "You didn't have to add - as a friend," Paul had texted.

"I was just playing it safe," Zarah replied. "Didn't want you to think I was clingy."

"No worries, Paul replied.

Eduard arrived to pick up Christy; and Zarah ran down stairs to get a lift into the school with them. Father had promised to pick her up later if she did not want to go home with Eduard and Christy, or if the couple were so disgustingly smoochy she could not bear their company. Benji didn't have a date and wasn't interested in dances at this stage. He looked surprised to see Zarah so dressed up.

"It's a school thing after all," Zarah said to her brother, shrugging her shoulders and attempting to appear casual. "You ought to think about it - Jeroma Tilton might have wanted to hang out with you."

"Nah," Benji dismissed the thought. "She's always all over Jaylen Woodgate."

"You know there's nothing in that," Zarah said. "They are practically related."

"You guys go on and have a good evening," Benji said. "I'm going to watch something on television."

Christy climbed into the front seat beside Eduard and placed a possessive hand upon his leg. Zarah climbed into the back seat and tried to pretend that she wasn't there. It was a very short distance to the school, where Eduard parked the car and they all piled out.

Christy linked her arm firmly in Eduard's and led him towards the dance floor as soon as they entered the hall. Zarah, who hadn't been to a school dance before, hovered in the doorway. After a few minutes she spied Paul waving to her from the balcony and climbed the small flight of stairs to join him.

"You look very nice," Paul said, as Zarah slid into the seat beside him.

"So do you," Zarah replied honestly. Paul Booth did scrub up remarkably well in a shirt and tie. She realized he was avoiding looking down her open neckline and giggled self-consciously. That was the opposite effect to the one she had hoped for, when she bought the dress and lacy push up brassiere. Well, she could hardly grab the boy's head and make him look closer.

"About the lady," Paul said in a low voice. "We agreed it was weird right? Do you think we should tell anyone?"

"Um, Wilson has this theory about them and us," Zarah said. "And he said the rats were an 'us' thing."

"The lady looked like one of them," Paul observed. "It doesn't fit."

"Unless," Zara mused, "She was a 'neither', like the Nevermores."

"So we tell Eduard then?" Paul suggested. "He is your sister's boyfriend and all that."

"I don't care what Christy says, Eduard is not an adult," Zara remarked sternly. "I say we tell his brother Damien."

"Damien hangs out with Captain Etheridge, who is close to the Sheriff," Paul remarked, "So that might just work."

"Agreed then," Zarah said. She began to relax and enjoy the night. "We will do it soon."

As Benji had predicted, Jeroma Tilton was hanging around Jaylen Woodgate. Jaylen was dividing his time between Jeroma, whom he clearly thought of as some sort of little cousin, and Bridget Etheridge, who rumor had it, he really fancied.

Javier Tilton was walking across the crowded dance floor, with his boots tapping on the boards, and his black coat swinging around his ankles. The coat was as long if not longer, than many of the girl's dresses. It was a 'Goth' thing, a fashion Javier had brought with him when he had moved to Mystic Evermore from Chicago.

Javier walked up to where Carlice Favor was bopping with Fenton Etheridge and tapped Fenton on the shoulder. Javier clearly meant to cut in, but Fenton managed not to look offended. Carlice Favor laughed and linked up with Javier, who led her into a slow dance, while others discoed around them. Trust Javier to insist on being different.

Carlice Favor was popular and Javier clearly knew better than to monopolize her time. When they passed by her ex-boyfriend Jaylen, he stopped and let her go. Carlice and Jaylen then linked up and commenced to hustle for old time's sake.

Everyone at Mystic Evermore High knew Javier Tilton was looking for a girlfriend and thoroughly enjoying the looking process. He even led sensible Anna Vaughn onto the dance floor and kept her there throughout several songs.

"You didn't want to dance, did you?" Paul was looking really embarrassed.

Zarah shook her head. "Maybe later," she said. "But this is my first time, and I don't think I can."

"I know exactly what you mean," Paul sounded relieved. "Say, look over there, is your sister okay?"

Christy was sitting on the edge of the dance area fuming as Eduard led his ex-girlfriend Lena Lenore onto the dance floor.

"She should be able to take that in good grace," Zarah remarked. "Everyone is circulating tonight."

"She needs to be a good sport," Paul observed, "But she looks as though she's had some spiked punch or something."

Zarah looked closer, and noticed Christy did indeed look flushed. The song finished and Eduard returned Lena to her seat.

He went to the refreshment table and collected two glasses of mineral water for himself and Christy, who was his official date for the evening.

Javier Tilton, who was still on the make, pulled Lena onto the dance floor. Everyone saw Eduard stiffen and freeze half way through his return journey towards Christy. Rumor had it, that although Eduard was happy with Christy, he was still not cool with Javier putting the moves on Lena.

Lena and Javier circled the floor in a formal waltz. The music changed and Javier still did not let Lena go. Instead he tightened his hold. Zarah knew from rehearsals for the Mystic Evermore High Musical Extravaganza, which Javier would be accompanying upon the piano, that Javier Tilton had the soul of a showman. The fact that Eduard was irritated by Javier's display probably added spice to the boy's steps.

Lena did not appear to object to Javier's attentions, but Eduard put down the glasses of mineral water he had been carrying, and began walking across the dance floor towards the circling couple. The other couples swiveled to a standstill as the crowd held its' collective breath, waiting to see what would happen next between the two boys. A fight over Lena Lenore would be an exciting spectacle at an otherwise well chaperoned school social event.

Christy gave a smothered cry and a gasp. She leapt up and ran out of the school hall. Eduard turned from Lena and called out his girlfriend's name, "Christy". Christy merely ran faster into the darkness and trees behind the school. She crossed the road and headed on out of town.

Eduard began to run after her, calling to Jaylen and Jamie to circle around and cut her off. Christy was faster than anyone expected in her grief, and appeared not to understand Eduard was merely chasing her to apologize for his neglect. She ran wildly, and when she reached one of the southern river crossings, she stumbled and fell into the water. Although she landed near the bank, it was quite a drop. Christy's leg was twisted and her neck was crooked.

Jaylen ran back towards the school urging the students to follow no further. "There is nothing you want to see here," he said.

Eduard climbed down into the river and pulled Christy out. He carried her up to the bank and attempted to give her mouth to mouth resuscitation.

Someone had called the Sheriff and the ambulance, but the ambulance officers declared there was nothing they could do for Christy. They declared her dead on impact, placed the body on a trolley and wheeled it into the ambulance.

Zarah identified herself as Christy's sister. She climbed up into the ambulance alongside Eduard, and they were carried to the hospital with the lights flashing and sirens blaring. When they arrived at the hospital, the hospital staff asked whether Christy was an organ donor.

Zarah answered with a vehement "no," because the idea of her sister's body being carved up and patched into other people's bodies was abhorrent. Christy was then carried into a closed examination room to await transfer to the morgue.

Eduard and Zarah were sitting beside the corpse, waiting in stunned silence for the rest of the Strahan family to arrive, when Christy sighed.

"I'm so thirsty," the deceased teenager whispered, opening her eyes and staring around wildly.

Eduard cried out in remorse and alarm.

"I'm so sorry Christy, I would give the world for this not to have happened to you."

Christy's eyes focused on Eduard in anger. "You!" she cried. "You did this to me. I can sense what you are."

Eduard bent over Christy sobbing. "That kinky sort of making-out we did a few hours before the dance, has changed you," he choked out. "You tried biting me back, so you died with my blood in your system."

Christy was still looking at Eduard with horror in her eyes. "You are the same Edward Nevermore that used to go out with my grandmother," she exclaimed. "I can hear it in your thoughts. And to think I fell in love with you too. How disgusting!"

Eduard turned appealing eyes upon Zarah.

"Get Carlice Favor," he cried, "Tell her it's urgent. My brother Damien too, if you can find him. We need all the help we can get before your family arrive."

Christy began to struggle with Eduard. She broke his hold, and once again was off running. This time she was faster, although she was also weak from the change. Eduard followed her around the hospital and out into the street.

Zarah walked out into the hospital car park, where she was allowed to turn her mobile phone back on again. She had Carlice Favor's number from school.

Carlice was still at the dance, but she agreed to come as quickly as possible, although with Christy on the run, no one knew exactly where to go.

"Bridget can get Damien for you too," Carlice suggested, "I'll just give her a yell".

Luckily Christy was disoriented and circled back around to the hospital, where Eduard was able to catch up with her. He was holding her by the shoulders, firmly, but with lover-like gentleness.

"Where can we go that is quiet?" Eduard asked Zarah. "She will need to be under cover when morning comes too."

"Go to the shop," Zarah suggested. "There is a loft above the store room. It has a couch and a few things, even its own bathroom. But it's rarely used. And it's all barred and lockable like the rest of the store, because Grandmother had some trouble with youths breaking in after the medicines a few years ago."

"Okay," Eduard said, "Lead the way."

Fortunately Damien Nevermore drove up just then, with Carlice in his car. Damien's vintage Plymouth had been blown up after his Uncle Sebastian's wedding, so now he was driving an Oldsmobile. It was a marvel how they had been so quick, afterwards Damien said he had been restless, on the prowl almost, and had taken the car out for a drive.

Damien wasn't proud to admit it, but knowing that two of the girls he cared about (ex-girlfriend Bridget Etheridge and his brother's former girlfriend Lena Lenore) were at the school having a good time unsettled him. The thought that the girls were possibly hooking up with other males, had turned him slightly stalky.

So although Bridget had promised Damien solemnly she would not take Jaylen Woodgate's courtship seriously, he was parked almost opposite the school hall when Carlice's text reached him.

"What's up man?" Damien cried. He whistled when he saw the wild eyed Christy in Eduard's arms.

Carlice leapt out and opened the back door of the car for Eduard and Christy. "Put Zarah in the front," she hissed urgently, before climbing in the back seat with Eduard and Christy.

Christy was struggling in Eduard's arms and appeared to be trying to get at Zarah, but not in a sisterly way.

"Drive," Carlice cried urgently. "Christy can smell warm blood."

"Where too?" Damien asked. "Woodgate Estate?"

"No that's a bit brutal," Eduard said. "Strahan's store. Apparently there's a secure area upstairs. If she's coming through this, she needs comfortable surroundings."

"Is coming through this even a good thing?" Zarah inquired.

Eduard shook his head. "No," he said. "But now we have the choice of two evils. Either Christy lives as a vampire, or she dies forever. Moreover, she has to be kept from killing a human in the next twenty four hours, or we might have to stake her."

"Staking," Zarah realized, "Was what we did to those rats!"

"Yeah," Damien said somewhat bitterly. "Just like the rats. How does it feel to be the only human in a car full of vampires, Zarah?"

"What!" Zarah exclaimed. "You are all vampires? Carlice too - she's at school with me!"

"I met with an unfortunate accident," Carlice said. "And I don't kill humans. Nor do the Nevermore brothers nowadays. They have learned over the years to control their blood lust. That's what Christy has to learn if she is ever to rejoin Mystic Evermore society, or any other human settlement again."

"We've arrived at the store," Damien announced. "Does anyone have a key? It would save me breaking in."

"I have a spare," Zarah said and scrambled out of the car. The other's followed and she led the way around to the rear of the store and unlocked the metal door in the loading bay.

"Very handy," Damien said, "I would hate to have to walk through the glass. It wouldn't hurt me that much, but would be very messy."

"And set the alarms off," Zarah observed. She was beginning to appreciate Damien's rather dry sense of humor, although before this she had always found the elder Nevermore brother intimidating.

"As this is a store, do we need an invitation to enter?" Carlice murmured. "I usually walk right in the front door because it says 'Welcome' in green light."

"The back area may be classed as a residence," Eduard said. "I've never been around here."

"I invite you all in," Zarah said impatiently. "There it's done."

Eduard and Carlice half carried Christy upstairs, and laid her down on the couch in the loft. As Zarah had described, the windows were barred to prevent access from the outside, but it would do almost as well to prevent escape from the inside. By now Christy was half faint from thirsting for blood and lay down more docilely.

"She needs to feed if she's going to survive," Carlice said. She pulled a medical blood bag out of her purse. "It's gross what I walk around with sometimes."

"Are we agreed we let her live as a vampire?" Damien asked.

Eduard nodded. "She was my girlfriend. I don't want to be responsible for killing her twice."

"From personal experience," Carlice observed, "I'd rather have some life as a vampire, than no life at all."

"She was my sister," Zarah cried, "Keep her alive if you can."

"It's not real life," Damien warned. "And my personal experience isn't as positive as Carlice's. Still, you are the next of kin here. It's your call."

"Try to save her, please," Zarah said. "And try to teach her not to kill, if that is what is required."

"Well here goes," Carlice said and handed the bag of medical blood to Christy. Christy tore the bag open and guzzled its contents greedily.

"I feel weird," Christy announced when she had finished the blood bag.

"You are changing," Carlice said. "Your life will never be the same again."

"Tell me something I don't know," Christy responded gloomily.

"I can teach you a thing or two," Carlice said. "I have been a vampire for a while now."

There was the sound of footsteps down below, the footfalls were too faint for Zarah's human hearing, but all the vampires could hear with their over-sensitive ears.

"Someone is in the store," Eduard exclaimed. "You locked the door again didn't you Zarah?"

"Yes I did," Zarah said. "Go and see who it is please Damien."

Damien descended the stairs and crossed the store room. They heard the muffled sound of his greeting someone gently. He called back upstairs in a slightly louder voice. "It's Esmeralda Strahan, shall I bring her up?"

"Yes do," Eduard called.

Zarah was already descending the stairs. "What are you doing here so early on a Sunday morning, Grandmother?" she cried.

"We heard the bad news and your parents are at the hospital while the staff are trying to find the body," Grandmother Strahan replied. "But I know you Zarah! You love the store and you would come here if anything happened. You are like me in that."

"Oh Grandma," Zarah cried.

Then Damien Nevermore did the strangest thing. He knelt down on one knee before Grandma Strahan as if he were about to propose. He clasped one of her hands in both of his and looked deep into her eyes. "Something bad has finally happened, Ezzie," he whispered.

Years of memory appeared to return to Grandma Strahan in the gentlest possible way, perhaps because they had merely been modified and not erased.

"You look just the same as ever Darren Nevermore," Grandmother whispered.

"They all call me Damien now," Damien said gently.

"Damien is it?" Grandmother Strahan repeated. "How quaint! Is Edward here?"

"Upstairs with Christy," Damien said. "You have kept your family safe from the pointy teeth creatures for years."

"I have too, haven't I?" Grandmother Strahan looked proud of herself.

"But now your Granddaughter Christy has become a pointy teeth thing herself," Damien explained. "Ezzie, you must be very brave."

Grandmother Strahan looked stern. "How did that happen Darren?" she asked.

"Christy bit Edward," Damien said.

Grandmother Strahan marched up the stairs two at a time, an amazing feat at her age.

"Christy," she pronounced sternly. "I hear you have been a naughty girl. I understand having a bit of fun and allowing your vampire boy-friend to give you a couple of love-bites, I did that too in my day. But biting him back was always where I drew the line. Bad things happen if you bite them back."

"I'm so sorry, Grandma," Christy gasped in amazement. "I love you."

"I love you too," Grandmother Strahan gathered her vampire descendant into her arms despite Carlice's desperate warnings. "Don't you bite me, Christy-girl!"

"No Grandma," Christy said, although she was white and shaking with the effort to restrain herself. "Please let me go."

Grandmother Strahan turned to Eduard. "Edward, you ought to have known better!"

"I'm sorry, Ezzie," Eduard exclaimed. "She was so insecure and she begged."

"It was time to break it off then," Grandmother Strahan said. "Better to be single than in an emotional mess."

"Christy and I didn't see it that way at the time," Eduard said.

"You were serious about her then," Grandmother Strahan said. "But your judgement was always a little weak, Edward. It took me to be the strong one when the time came to decide our future."

"You asked Darren to glamour your memories so you could live a normal life," Eduard reminisced. "I hated him for doing that."

"You hated your brother for a lot of silly reasons," Grandmother Strahan observed.

"Well, he had no right interfering," Eduard retorted.

"I would have asked the same for my Granddaughter too if I had known things were going this poorly between the two of you," Grandmother Strahan insisted. "Christy didn't know what you were, and was out of her mind with jealousy. It was a fault I counselled her against. Still what is done, is done now. We have got to work out what sort of life she can have in the future."

"About the same as mine, if she can learn control," Carlice suggested.

"That's something at least," Grandma Strahan sighed.

"Christy's never had a lot of control," Zarah ventured. Her sister glared at her.

"Shut up Zarah," Christy snapped. "I've worked out you were right about Eduard, but I've had a nasty shock and this is not the time to say 'I told you so'."

"Christy will be alright now," Grandmother Strahan said protectively. "She has Carlice and she has me. Darren please take Zarah back to the hospital to collect her parents and work out some sort of cover story to tell them about Christy."

****

Zarah reluctantly followed Damien Nevermore downstairs to the car. The adrenaline triggered by the crisis was fading, leaving her filled with grief. Even if her sister succeeded in making life as a vampire, she would never be the same again.

"What will happen now?" she asked.

"Carlice and your Gran will attempt to comfort your sister through the first few days or even weeks of vampire life," Damien explained. "If Christy can control the blood-lust she can return to your home and family. It's up to her. Some vampires choose to go away from home and start anew where no one knows them."

"What will we tell Mum and Dad?" Zarah asked.

"I've been thinking about that," Damien said. "Best to tell your parents that Christy was moved somewhere else for treatment because one of the doctors thought there was hope."

"That sounds good," Zarah said. "And it leaves things open, when we know what really happens, we will give Mum and Dad an update."

They drove in silence for a moment, and then Zarah spoke. "I've been forgetting, there was something I wanted to talk to you about." She stumbled through Wilson's theory of "them" and "us" and seeing the lady making a pet out of the vampire rats.

"The lady sounds remarkably like an ancestral vampire, or one of their cronies," Damien remarked at the end of the recital. "They sometimes come back here to make trouble. You have done the right thing in telling me."

"Will you tell the Sheriff?" Zarah asked.

"I might take Captain Etheridge with me and check things out," Damien said. "The Captain is a remarkably good man in a tight spot. Now, I need to drop you here and you need to go to your parents. Christy will need more blood, so I have to pay a visit to the hospital stores... and I can't exactly just walk in and ask for blood... if you know what I mean."

"Err... yes," Zarah stammered. "Well thanks for all your help tonight."

Zarah left the car and walked across the hospital car park, up the stairs and in through the front door. Her parents were seated near the emergency desk wearing anxious expressions on their faces. They rose to their feet when they saw Zarah.

"Where have you been?" cried Barbara. "The hospital has lost Christy's body and no one will tell us anything."

"Mum, Dad," Zarah begged, "Can we please go home? I am exhausted."

"As there seems to be nothing we can do here," Robbie remarked, "We may as well go home and take care of Zarah and Benji."

"What about Christy?" Barbara cried once again, but she allowed herself to be led towards the car park.

Once outside the front door, Robbie turned to Zarah, "Explain yourself girl," he said. "We were told you rode the ambulance in here with Christy's body and you must know something."

"Yes Dad," Zarah began to cry. "I did come in here with the ambulance, and we were sent to a room to wait for you. While we were there a different Doctor came in and he said there might be some hope for Christy. She was taken elsewhere for treatment."

"Without telling us or anything?" Barbara's tone was stern. "We are her parents."

"Granny arrived and went with her," Zarah said with a sudden flash of inspiration.

Barbara relaxed visibly. "Your mother is quite capable," she murmured to Robbie. "I'm sure she will see Christy gets the best treatment available."

The Strahan family got into the car and Robbie drove home. He parked in the drive way and escorted his wife into the house before pulling his daughter aside for a private word.

"Don't tell Mum," he whispered, "But I think the hospital staff must have been hallucinating. One told me Christy had died of a broken neck, while another swore they saw her run out of the hospital!"

"Imagine that!" Zarah murmured.

Zarah was emotionally and physically exhausted and dropped straight into bed. When she woke up later that day, there were messages on her mobile phone. Carlice assured her that all was as well as it could be. A number of school friends sent inquiries about Christy's health that Zarah did not know how to answer.

Finally, there was a message from Paul Booth that said: "What happened last night? I saw you go off in the ambulance and waited till this morning to ask."

Zarah hesitated over the phone, and then she typed: "Can you keep a secret? I have something to tell you. Meet later."

A few minutes later, her phone beeped. "You can trust me. I've something to tell you too. Paul."

Zarah turned over in bed and settled down to catch a few more hours sleep. She woke about one o'clock, showered and dressed.

Barbara had been too distressed to cook a proper lunch, but there were left-overs to warm in the oven and Zarah dined quite well. Grandmother had returned to the Strahan house and confirmed Zarah's cover story. There was a slim chance Christy could recover, but she needed extensive treatment. She needed complete quiet now, and the following therapy was so specialized she had been sent to Atlanta.

Christy would receive some experimental nerve treatment at first and then possibly months of physiotherapy. The Strahan parents accepted the story and even the poor excuse why they could not visit their daughter. Any alternative explanation would have been unbearable.

Grandmother Strahan had been by the Mystic Evermore Hospital and collected Christy's things. She handed Zarah Christy's verbena infused silver pendant.

"The hospital staff took it off her last night," Grandmother explained. "Christy would like you to wear it as a small protection against harm."

"Eduard gave that to her," Zarah objected.

"She cannot wear it now," Grandmother said practically. "The silver hurts her neck."

Unbuttoning her own blouse, Grandmother peeled back the 'peter pan' collar to reveal a peace symbol hanging around her neck. It was composed of an outer circle and upside down 'V' shape in the center.

"Very popular in my day," Grandmother said. The peace symbol was also made from silver and had a distinctive aroma like Verbena. "Great-Grandma Booth made this for me years ago, when I was at school with her daughter."

Zarah accepted the simple star Christy used to wear. It was made out of two triangles and sometimes known as the 'star of David'. The Strahan family may have had a Jewish ancestor at some time and Christy had always been very fond of the motif.

"For Christy," Zarah murmured as she placed it around her neck.

Paul Booth arrived around two in the afternoon riding his bicycle. "I'm sorry, I don't drive yet," he admitted somewhat shame-faced. "Wilson only drives because your father got him his license to work for the business."

"I don't have my learners' permit yet either," Zarah said. "Next year, I'll go for it."

Although she was still very tired, Zarah hauled her bicycle out of the garage and dusted it off. It had been a few weeks since she last ridden it but the chain still spun smoothly. "Let's go," she said.

The wind in her hair was exhilarating and Zarah could feel it blowing the sleep out of her head. 'If only grief could be blown away as easily', she thought.

They only rode as far as the park down by the river near the community garden. This was the opposite direction from where Christy had run and fallen last night, but Zarah still shuddered at the thought of crossing the bridge.

Paul and Zarah threw their bikes down on the grass and sat down on the benches in the Japanese garden area. No one else was near. The few keen gardeners out that day were busy tilling their individual plots.

Zarah had chosen the bench that placed her back to the river, from there she could see the road and across the road, the cemetery. She shivered. Paul put an arm around her in a non-demanding sort of comforting manner.

"Tell me Zarah," he whispered.

Zarah was silent for a moment. It seemed she had known Paul Booth forever and hung out with him at school without barely noticing. Wilson Booth had been more exotic and appealing to a young girl's eye. And yet, here she was, knowing she would only ever be 'just good friends' with Wilson Booth, and about to pour her heart out to his brother Paul.

Moving on was much easier than it had seemed when she first contemplated it. Wilson had liked Christy, and after what had happened, Zarah didn't think she could ever look at a boy who had liked Christy. Even if he was a nice guy.

"Christy died last night..." she whispered into Paul's arm.

"And yet, rumor has it she could recover..." Paul murmured.

"She woke up again," Zarah choked. "Asking for blood."

"She became a vampire," Paul concluded.

"Yeah," Zarah sobbed. "Apparently there are vampire people as well as vampire bats. Some of them are taking care of Christy. If she can learn not to kill humans, she might be able to come back to us."

"The probability of a vampire wanting to live a normal human life is really pretty low," Paul murmured.

"Why not?" Zarah exclaimed. "I met some that did."

"The Nevermores are the exception, not the norm," Paul explained. "The Agrarian Council has a truce with the good vampire community managed by Elisha Blackermore, although there is some disagreement as to which ones are 'good'."

"I'll bet," Zarah muttered. "How do you know all this?"

"I promised to tell you a secret too," Paul said. "I am a Booth."

"I knew that," Zarah almost giggled. Then it began to sink in. "Like Great-Grandma and Raven?"

Great-Grandma Booth was rumored to have been a 'witch' while she was alive. The locals had visited her to buy home-made cough mixtures and other reasonably innocent New Age remedies. Some purchased good luck-charms, like Grandmother Strahan's peace necklace. The occasional desperate person asked for a curse or a love potion, but it was rumored Great-Grandma Booth refused to supply either.

Her great-granddaughter, Raven, had recently come out as a 'Hudu' worker, which was almost an accepted cultural practice nowadays. The word 'Hudu' was originally the name of an African language. In modern times it was a folk practice that combined African traditional and Christian thought, focusing on miracles like those performed by the Hebrew-Egyptian patriarch Moses.

It probably wasn't the correct term for a natural born witch, but it was the one Raven had chosen.

"Just like Great-Grandma and Raven," Paul said. "Although maybe not as powerful as Raven. I do not know yet."

"Mm," Zarah mused. It was a lot to take in. "Do you think you could help my sister?"

"I don't know," Paul said. "I really haven't practiced my powers... you know my father has a bad heart?"

"Yes," Zarah replied, fascinated.

"He is like that because he burnt himself out," Paul said. "He took too much power in trying to battle evil one night. He's always insisted I never do that."

"Funny I've never seen Wilson do anything or say anything," Zarah murmured.

"Wilson can't," Paul said. "He is not a true Booth."

"What?" Zarah exclaimed.

"Mother was pregnant when she met Father," Paul said. "She immediately knew he was the love of her life and married him. Her old boyfriend left town with another woman, and it was never any big deal. Dad still loved Wilson when he was born and he has always been my brother. But he is not a true Booth and he doesn't have any witch powers that I know of."

"What can you do?" Zarah asked.

"Do you trust me?" Paul said. "Enough to come across into the cemetery with me?"

"Sure," Zarah said. The teenagers had one proper bike lock between them, so they hooked the chain between the spokes of the front wheels on both bikes and locked them to the leg of the stone bench in the Japanese garden.

Paul took Zarah by the hand and led her across the road to the cemetery. They by-passed all the modern graves and entered the old section. Here several graves had been built up into vault-like tombs. Paul pushed on the door to one of the vaults and it opened.

"The Keels were one of the pioneer families," Zarah murmured.

"We aren't doing any harm," Paul said. "I just need the dark." He reached out his hand in front of them and a small ball of light appeared in his palm. Someone had left candles in a niche on the monument and Paul guided the light toward the candle. He lit the candle and then extinguished the little ball of light.

"There did you see?" Paul asked, anxious to hear Zarah's response.

"I did," Zarah said. "I think you are remarkable. So controlled too."

"I have always practiced keeping my spells small," Paul said. "One of the first things Dad did when he came into his powers was nearly set himself on fire! I have always been determined to maintain control."

"I see," Zarah said. "Can we go outside again now?" She didn't really like it inside the tomb.

"Okay," Paul said. He turned to extinguish the candle and something glinted in its flame "What's that over there?"

"Eyes! Reflecting in the light," Zarah cried. "Please let's go."

"If we are lucky, it's a neighborhood cat," Paul said.

"It's not a cat, it's one of those rats," Zarah exclaimed. She grabbed Paul by the hand and began stumbling towards the steps. "Leave the candle, it will burn itself out and do no harm."

"There are more rats," Paul observed. He raised his hand. "They are coming out from the back of the tomb. I will give them a headache so they won't follow us."

Zarah was too frightened to watch what Paul was doing, but the glowing eyes seemed to close and small bodies thumped to the ground behind them. The teenagers scrambled up the steps and out of the tomb. Paul secured the door.

"Did you kill them?" Zarah panted.

"I don't know," Paul replied. "They may be merely stunned. You know the only true way to kill those pointy toothed rats is a wooden stake straight through the heart."

How do you know that?" Zarah inquired.

"I've seen Wilson and your Father," Paul remarked. "And some knowledge - folk tales really - gets passed down through the Booth family. Some of it is true and useful, some of it is not."

"Are we safe now? I'm dying to catch my breath," Zarah asked.

"They won't come out into the sun," Paul assured her. "We have been safe ever since we shut the door."

"Oh!" Zarah breathed, looking around the cemetery which suddenly did not seem like an empty shell of gravestones and mourning chapels anymore. "If it's alright with you, I'd like to find our bikes."

"Sure," Paul said. They were almost at the gates. Once outside, they paused and checked the traffic, before crossing the road in regulation fashion. As Paul said, he liked to maintain control and he would not allow panic to overcome his sense of safety.

The Japanese garden seemed tranquil and inviting. Zarah threw herself down on the grass. She lay there drinking in the sweet scents of flowers and nearby garden patches. Someone had been watering their plants and a faint scent of mud mingled with the other aromas.

"It's so good to be free," Zarah stretched her arms out.

Paul sat down beside her. "Are you alright?" he asked.

"Yeah," Zarah said. "I just hated the tomb."

"I'm sorry I took you in there," Paul was contrite.

"It's not your fault." Zarah said. "I've had a lot of shocks lately, starting with Christy..."

"Your boyfriend being a witch," Paul murmured.

"Nah, I'm not so bothered by that," Zarah said. "I've always known about Great-grandma Booth, she was a nice lady and friend of my Grandma's. What did you say - 'boyfriend'?"

"Boy-who-is-a-friend," Paul was scarlet beneath his dusky complexion.

"Yeah you better have meant that," Zarah said. "Because you haven't actually asked me yet."

Paul's face suddenly blocked out the sunlight and he placed a kiss upon Zarah's lips. His hands rested the ground on either side of her head. Although his hair was cropped close, she noticed it had a natural wave.

"Boy-who-is-a-friend and wants to kiss you when you are

scared," he said. "Is that better?"

"I'll think about it," Zarah was going to resist, but then she reached her arms up and around his body, pulling him down onto her. Any further conversation was lost in each other's mouths and the delight of feeling another person's body pressing against theirs. After a few minutes, the teens rolled apart. Both were panting and their hearts were racing.

"I didn't know it could be like that," Paul murmured.

"I feel we are very young," Zarah whispered. "I hadn't imagined getting a boyfriend before my senior year."

"If you're lucky," Paul said, "I'll still be around next year." He pulled Zarah to her feet and sat on the bench to unlock their bikes. "I guess we better go and find some adults to tell about the rats."

"I told Damien Nevermore last night," Zarah remarked. "He said he would be getting Captain Etheridge involved."

"Captain Etheridge, Damien Nevermore, the cops and the fire-brigade, I should think. If the rats are plaguing it will take quite a team to clear them all out," Paul observed.

"I hadn't thought of the police as pest exterminators," Zarah mused.

Paul laughed. "Whatever else do you think they are?" he said. "Although the easiest way to get rid of the rats would be to kill their sire. Then the rest would simply fade away."

"What do you mean - sire?" Zarah asked.

"The first vampire rat would have made the others," Paul said. "You don't think they breed like normal rats, do you?"

"I dunno," Zarah said. "I don't suppose so."

****

Monday at school, Zarah faced many awkward questions from her classmates who wanted to know what had really happened to Christy, and how she was recovering. Zarah told them all that she did not know the details, which she assured herself was the truth. For once she was glad when her brother Benji joined the class for mathematics and science. Benji was grieving just as badly as Zarah was, but at least his ignorance was genuine, and Zarah could hide behind its comforting bulwark.

The most awkward questions came from the members of

Christy's class, some of whom had been at the dance and seen a little of what happened. The very hardest person to answer was Christy's best friend, Ivy Pinkerton who was clearly genuine in her concern. Zarah could not handle this and burst into tears, which was effective in stopping most of the seniors from asking more questions. Ivy, however, remained behind to comfort Zarah as she cried.

"Oh Ivy," Zarah sobbed, and Ivy threaded an arm around her shoulders.

"It's alright," Ivy whispered. "I know it's not really alright, with Christy gone, but it is okay to cry. I'll tell the others to leave you alone."

Zarah longed to share her burden with Ivy. She tried to think about Ivy's family and wondered whether they were as perfect, and ignorant about the vampire problem in Mystic Evermore as they seemed. After all, Paul had been remarkably well informed and even harboring a secret of his own, but then... he was a Booth. Zarah honestly couldn't tell whether it was safe to tell Ivy and could not take the risk in confiding in the older girl.

Eduard was not at school that day, which was just as well. The students had mixed opinions of his behavior after Saturday night. Some were inclined to be sympathetic towards him because he had lost his girlfriend to the accident. Others were inclined to blame him for driving Christy to it. The unsettling rumor that Christy jumped, rather than fell into the river began to circulate amongst the students who held Eduard responsible for the incident.

Lena and Javier were keeping their heads down and appeared to be concentrating on the school work. Everyone agreed they could not be held responsible for the accident. All they did was dance together, and Eduard chose to make (or almost make, as it turned out) a resentful scene about it. Christy's jealousy issues were surely between her and Eduard too. Lena was merely moving on by dancing with other guys, and Javier was a completely free agent.

Carlice was at school and she helped steer the seniors away from gossip about Christy. She could not reveal she had any special knowledge, but she assured the seniors that Zarah's account was correct and begged them not to pressure Zarah any further during her time of grief.

Paul Booth was a great support throughout the day. He did not sit with Zarah every class, but she caught his concerned eye watching over her. During one of the classes that Benji did not share with her, Zarah slid into the seat beside Paul just for the sheer relief of sitting beside someone who understood for an hour.

However, Zarah did not want the class talking about her commencing a new relationship immediately after Christy's accident, so she played it casual around Paul. Paul seemed content to follow her lead, and Zarah could not be sure that their kiss on the grass had been anything more than an experiment. It had been pleasant, and she longed for its repetition someday, but they had not exactly declared their undying love. Paul had only said he might be around next year... when she was ready. She hoped he meant it.

After school, Zarah walked across to Grandma's store as usual. Her heart smote her as she thought about seeing Christy; and she wondered whether Christy would be back to her old self, or still ravening for human blood. She was going to walk through the store, into the back room and up the stairs, but Grandmother shook her head. Then the older woman handed the till over to Zarah's mother, Barb, and accompanied Zarah into the staff-only area of the pharmacy where they could talk in private.

"Don't disturb Christy," Grandmother Strahan whispered. "She needs to sleep during the day, and there are too many people in the store. It would cause her unnecessary distress to awaken and sense them. Damien will arrive later to help Eduard transport her to the Woodgate Estate."

"The Woodgate Estate?" Zarah queried. "I heard talk of that the other night, but I wouldn't have thought Jaylen was one of the vampires. He always seems too warm... animal almost."

"You are right there," Grandmother agreed. "The Woodgate family does carry a special gene, but it's not for vampirism! Anyway, amongst the old buildings on the Woodgate Estate is an intact cellar, which Jaylen Woodgate has set up as his personal camp and home-away-from-home. Christy will be safe there."

"What if Jaylen wants to use it?" Zarah asked.

Grandmother Strahan shrugged. "Jaylen only uses it during the full moon, so Christy will be safe there for another two weeks at least."

"Will you visit her there?" Zarah asked.

Grandmother Strahan looked sad. "I don't know," she said. "I haven't been able to help Christy as much as I had hoped. She still hates Eduard, but he is the only one who has been able to manage her. Carlice too sometimes, but it was decided Carlice should still go to school. She wants very much to graduate this year like a normal girl."

"So did Christy," Zarah choked. "Until she met Eduard."

"Try not to think that way," Grandmother Strahan urged. "What happened - happened. I need you to do something for me though. I think it would be better coming from you."

"Anything I can do to help, Grandmother," Zarah breathed.

"Talk to your young friend Jamie Lenore," Grandmother Strahan said. "He skipped school today and came here. He said he could sense a new vampire in town. I told him Eduard Nevermore was upstairs and he went away, but he will be back I'm sure."

"Jamie Lenore," Zarah breathed. That muscle-bound delinquent everybody was so fond of, because he lost his aunt and uncle in a car crash the other year. Lena Lenore's younger cousin and her sometimes classmate. She had been so busy coping that she had hardly noticed he was absent from school that day.

"The Lenore's held a very special place on the original Agrarian Council," Grandmother said, switching into gossip mode once again. "But they have never been as snobby as some."

Zarah laughed. Since her memory had been rejuvenated, Grandma's gossip had gained a little spice. She pulled out her mobile phone to work out how she could get hold of Jamie Lenore and noticed she had a message. It was from Paul asking whether she was alright and if she wanted him to come over later. That also made her smile.

She typed a text to Carlice. "Need to talk to Jamie Lenore," it said.

"Uh-oh, should have thought of that!" Carlice's reply came quickly. "I think he went around to Ravens' place. She was due back yesterday."

"Okay," Zarah texted. "What time are you guys moving Christy tonight?"

"After dark of course!" Carlice replied.

"Can I come?" Zarah asked.

"I dunno," Carlice replied. "I'll ask Damien. If not tonight, he may take you tomorrow."

Zarah stared at her phone thoughtfully for a few minutes and then typed a text to Paul. "Come over on your bike. We need to visit Raven."

The reply came soon after. "Be there in ten."

Zarah walked the short distance from the store to her house and changed out of her school uniform into leggings, which were much more convenient for riding the bike. There was a soft swish of bike tires on the gravel and Paul knocked on the door. Zarah was so pleased to see him, she impulsively gave him a big hug.

Paul looked pleased: "So you weren't giving me the cold shoulder at school, then," he said.

"No, never," Zarah replied. "I'm not like that. But I am a bit private and I didn't want people talking about us as well as Christy."

"Okay, I thought about that too," Paul said, "They will notice sometime if we keep hanging out."

"Our families have been friends for ages, and Wilson works for my Dad," Zarah said. "It might take them a while to notice... and anytime that is not so close to the accident would be better."

"As you say," Paul agreed. "Now what are we seeing Raven about? I thought she was out of town this term."

"It's Jamie Lenore, we really have to see," Zarah said, hopping on her bike. "Come on let's go."

"Little Lenore, eh?" Paul pedaled after her.

Everyone knew where Great-Grandma Booth's cottage had been on the edge of town. It was logical to assume Raven had returned there, even though she had been devastated by the loss of her great-grandmother. Paul and Zarah made good time on their bikes and were soon riding up the driveway.

The house was quiet, but they walked up to the front door and Zarah knocked. No response. Zarah knocked again.

Raven Booth opened the door. She was a pretty dark girl with a fine nose and good cheekbones framed by short curly hair. "I'm sorry," she said. "I'm just back from my trip. I didn't know anyone knew."

She eyed Paul and Zarah curiously.

"We need to speak to Jamie," Zarah said. "Carlice suggested he might be here."

"Let them in, Raven," Jamie called. He appeared in the

passageway. His shirt was unbuttoned and the muscles on his chest rippled as he moved his arms. The expression on his face was slightly guilty, and Zarah deduced he and Raven Booth were an item in secret! The cover-up would make sense as he was a couple of years her junior. The kids at school were very particular about that sort of thing.

"Come in Zarah," Raven said stepping aside. "Paul."

Zarah entered the cottage and glanced around. It looked as though Raven had altered very little since her great-grandmother had passed. "I'm sorry about your great-grandmother," she said. "She was good friends with my Gran too."

"I will always miss my Grans," Raven said. "She was everything to me." A tear hovered in her eye. "Sometimes I feel she is still near me too."

Paul had been hesitating to enter the cottage, but he took a deep breath and stepped across the threshold. As he did so, several bells rang.

Raven jumped. "The witch alarm," she cried. "We are under attack."

Jamie grabbed up the nearest implement which happened to be the soup ladle, but he managed to make it look deadly. "Where?" He looked around wildly.

Paul held up his hands: "Peace," he said. "I am a Booth too. Raven's third cousin, descended from Great-Grandmother Booth's brother."

Jamie relaxed and put the soup ladle down onto the table where it turned back into an inoffensive cooking utensil. Raven looked her relative up and down sharply.

"We are only very distantly connected," she said.

"Yes, but I bred true," Paul said. "As did my father before me."

"When did it start for you?" Raven asked.

"Sometime last year," Paul said. "I expected it. We Booths usually come into our powers in our teens."

"I didn't expect anything," Raven said. "It was an awful shock and took me a while to accept. I hadn't ever even believed Great-Grandma was a witch - despite all this." She gestured around the room which displayed books on herbs and home remedies, and the shelf of silver jewelry making tools. "I thought these were her hobbies, quaint remnants of the seventies."

Paul coughed awkwardly. "I am truly sorry about your great-grandmother."

"So am I," Raven exclaimed. "And I blame myself, she would not have taken on levels of power above her capacity if I had not started the spell." She did not elaborate regarding what she and her great-grandmother had been attempting to achieve, but Paul looked understanding.

"My father went through something similar," Paul, murmured. "He lives, but he is a mere shell of himself. It strained his heart amongst other things."

"You said you needed to speak to me," Jamie said somewhat impatiently. He was looking at Zarah intently.

"Yeah, well my Gran said you came by the store today," Zarah replied. "And you tried to go upstairs."

"That's right," Jamie said. "You wanna tell me what's going on?"

Zarah began to cry. "I don't know how you knew, but my sister Christy turned into a vampire when she fell down the river-bank the other night. She died, but she woke up again and she wasn't the same. Eduard and Carlice are trying to teach her how to control the blood lust and not to kill people."

"And you want me not to kill your sister I guess?" Jamie sighed.

"That would be nice," Zarah said. "At least give her a chance. She has already died once."

Jamie sighed and flexed his arms. The biceps and triceps bulged and the movement rippled along his shoulders. Although she was becoming quite sure Paul was the boy for her, Zarah could not help looking. Raven noticed and frowned.

"I sometimes wonder what sort of town this is, that asks me to go against my instincts all the time and preserve their pet vampires," Jamie said. "Captain Etheridge is inconvenient with all his rules too. Saying, I'm not allowed to kill that fancy piece that moved into the old Mill Farm unless she does some harm too. Alright, you got it. I won't kill Christy unless she kills a human first."

"At least you've got that giant rat hunt the Sheriff and Captain Etheridge are organizing," Raven said.

"Vampire rats, woopy do," Jamie shrugged, but he looked more cheerful.

"They are quite scary, when there are a lot of them," Zarah said and described their experience in the tomb. "I do hope there are none in the cellars at the Woodgate Estate," she said remembering the plans to move Christy that evening.

"I expect Jaylen cleared them all out there last full moon," Jamie said.

"Of course," Zarah agreed. "I would set traps if it were my camping place."

Raven and Jamie both laughed. "Jaylen doesn't really need traps," Raven said, but she didn't explain any further.

Paul took Zarah by the hand. "I think we better be getting home now," he said. "Thanks Raven, thanks Jamie." He looked at Raven, "Those witch alarms sound handy. Perhaps you could show me how to make them sometime."

"Anything good, I'm willing to show you," Raven said, "But only white magic."

"Of course," Paul said. "I wouldn't want anything else." He didn't mention his rule about keeping it small either, but Zarah knew he was strict about that.

Paul dropped Zarah off at her house that evening and promised to see her the next day. Zarah's parents and brother Benji were still in mourning due to Christy's absence, and the house was quiet that evening. Carlice texted as promised to let Zarah and Grandmother know when the transfer between hiding places had been safely effected.

Zarah rose early Tuesday morning and got ready for school. She expected the second day would be easier and she would face less questions. Some students who had not heard the cover story yesterday might make inquiries, and Christies' best friends might ask whether she had heard anything from the sanitarium where Christy was supposedly residing for treatment.

It was a great comfort to know that Paul knew her secret. Lunch time Zarah sent a text to Carlice asking whether Damien would take her to see Christy that evening. Carlice returned the answer that she was very sorry, but it would be better if Zarah could wait a while to give Christy a chance to settle some more.

Wilson Booth dropped by the school that afternoon, driving Zarah's father's plumbing van. He explained that Zarah's father was working on a big job and her mother was at the general store. Zarah was happy to accept the ride home with Wilson, and ran to collect Benji from the locker area. Paul, who had ridden to school, was able to throw his bike in the back of the van.

"How have you kids been?" Wilson asked as he set the van into motion.

Zarah blushed. Her one-time crush was now treating her like a kid sister. A peek out of her eyelashes assured her that she was nothing like a kid sister to Paul, and she began to warm to the idea of a relationship with someone who considered her an equal.

"All right I suppose," she responded.

"School was the same as always," Paul said. Although he was the smart Booth, he did not try to pretend the school offered no challenges for an African-American boy. Indeed, there was almost no one who was not harassed about something at school. It was one of the disadvantages of the public education system.

"Have you been finding any more of them giant rats in the sewers?" Benji asked.

"Yeah everywhere," Wilson sighed. "Captain Etheridge and Damien's rat hunt can't come too soon for me."

"I found they responded to my special skills," Paul murmured discretely. "Zarah was with me at the time."

Wilson gave him a sharp look. "You know we don't really like you using your skills."

"I keep it small," Paul assured his brother.

Benji, who was not in on the Booth family secret, looked mildly puzzled.

"Ah - Wilson means that all juniors who join the rat hunt need to be accompanied by adults," Zarah dissembled.

"Oh of course," Benji appeared satisfied.

"Do you mind if we drop by home and check on Dad for a few?" Wilson said. This last was directed at Zarah and Benji.

"So long as my parents know where I am," Zarah said.

"I'm in no hurry to get home," Benji agreed.

Wilson took a slight detour into the poorer side of town and pulled up in front a neat two bedroom house. The kids jumped out of the plumber's van and Paul ran into the house.

"Dad," he cried, "We are here!"

John Booth appeared out of one of the bedrooms. He was weak and thin in comparison to his two healthy sons. He had been unable to hold a job for a few years and kept house for his two sons. Making ends meet as a single parent was a full-time job in itself, as some people would say. Things had been much easier for the entire family since Robbie Strahan had employed Wilson as his apprentice.

"Hello boys," John said. He appeared to be highly strung, sensitive and almost learned. "I applied for a job today," he said. "I might have got it, if Mrs. Woodgate, who was on the interview committee, was not so racist."

"What sort of job was it?" Paul asked.

"Caretaking and light maintenance of the Agrarian Council buildings," John said. "It's much like what I do around here and on my good days I am quite capable."

"And on your not-so-good days, you could re-schedule," Wilson announced cheerfully. "That's a great idea Dad!"

"Like I said," John Booth reiterated, "Everyone except Mrs. Woodgate really liked me. She thinks I'm not fit even to be her servant."

"Oh come on Dad," Paul exclaimed. "The Booths have been around Mystic Evermore nearly as long as the Woodgates."

"Ah yes, but Blacks were never allowed on the Agrarian Council," John Booth exclaimed.

"Neither were the Strahans," Benji said. "But our Dad always says that the rich and snobby need us."

"We won't repeat what else he says," Zarah added with a grin. "It involves toilets! Perhaps if our Dad gave you a reference?"

"I haven't really worked for him since I helped your Gran shift those boxes," John said.

"But that was something, Dad," Wilson said. "And if Mr. Strahan or Grandma Strahan were willing to give you a reference - it could swing the balance."

"Yeah," John Booth looked as though he bore the weight of many rejections on his shoulders. "Best thing I ever did was you boys!"

"Oh we agree Dad!" Wilson said cheekily. "Now I better get the two young Strahans to their home. Their father's got a few more hours work for me too."

"I'll see you later then Wilson," John said. "What would you like for tea Paul?"

"Goodbye Mr. Booth," Zarah said. "It was nice meeting you again."

Zarah could not remember whether they had been formally introduced before, so she was careful with her wording. Their Grandmothers might have been school friends, but Mystic Evermore was so rigidly stratified that one could live most of their life without mixing with residents from a different social group. It was only recently that some of the barriers appeared to have come down - and a few secrets had come to light as well!

"See you young Strahans," John Booth said. "Thank you for visiting."

Wilson drove Benji and Zarah back to their house and then continued to the plumbing job that he and Mr. Strahan were committed to working on.

When Zarah and Benji were alone at the house, Zarah, who was slightly older, was responsible for her brother. She instructed him to do his homework, before playing any computer games and went down to the kitchen to prepare a snack. It had once been Christy who took care of them, and Zarah missed her sister even though she had been bossy.

Zarah spread butter across the bread and cut generous chunks of meat, before adding cheese, sauce and salad. She was about to take one of the plates into the other room for Benji when she heard a scuffle in the kitchen cupboard, just under the sink.

Without thinking, Zarah opened the door. A rat hopped out of the dark space within the cupboard and she screamed. Benji came running to see what the noise was.

"It's one of those giant rats," Zarah cried.

Benji looked around wildly for something to hit the rat with and Zarah grabbed the bright torch her mother kept on top of the refrigerator. She shone it straight at the rat and the rodent froze, momentarily blinded by the light beam. Benji grabbed a metal crate designed to carry a number of milk cartons and dropped it over the rat to imprison it.

"Get a garden stake," Zarah instructed.

Benji headed for the back door, and then noticed his father had a box of wooden tomato stakes stored in the laundry. He selected one and returned to hover over the imprisoned rat.

"Be careful of your hands," Zarah said. "But pierce it straight through the chest if you can."

Benji missed several times and ended up with a couple of stakes sticking out of the rat's body at different points. This did not kill it, but did slow it considerably. Finally, Benji managed to aim straight through the chest. The rat fell down dead, before shimmering and disintegrating into dust.

Benji sat down on the kitchen floor and stared. "What was that – un-killable sort of rat? And why did Dad just happen to have the tomato stakes inside?" he asked. "It is like we are fighting vampires or something. There is more going on than you are telling me - isn't there?"

"Yeah there is," Zarah admitted. "Dad knows what to do because he has encountered the vampire rats down in the sewers."

"And that's what the big hunt will be about?" Benji inquired. "A plague of these across town."

"Something like that," Zarah said.

"If this were a computer game," Benji suggested, "There would be a point from where they were spawning."

"That is possible," Zarah said.

"So the hero would try to take out that point, or destroy the boss that was summoning them," Benji continued.

"In real life, we think there are hundreds of nests," Zarah said. "But your analogy could be helpful. Paul did suggest the rats had a sire."

"The rats don't seem - err natural," Benji speculated. "And there is the story they are telling at school - that Christy really died - and then got up again later. That doesn't seem very natural either."

He looked at Zarah sternly.

"You mustn't listen to the gossips," Zara protested.

"Some of these were Christy's best friends," Benji said. "They are not sure about anything anymore, but at first they were very clear. Christy's neck was definitely broken."

"Sit down," Zarah said. "If I tell you something, you must promise not to tell Mum and Dad. Or anyone else at school."

"Okay," Benji said. His eyes were wide. "Don't tell me we are really inside a virtual world where people can fall dead and wake up again with full health."

"No, but that would be cool!" Zarah began. "This town is real of course, but it is full of strange things… Dad half knows, but ignores in his practical - all men produce waste - sort of way… Granny used to know, but she forgot, and she is just beginning to remember… Mum of course, concentrates on the here and now."

"Go on," Benji was listening avidly. That was the trouble with having a super-smart younger brother. He was hard to fool.

"It turned out the Edward Nevermore that Grandma used to date, was the very same Eduard Nevermore Christy developed a crush on," Zarah explained.

"That would make him over sixty," Benji exclaimed. "And he looks our age."

"He is a vampire," Zarah continued. "And so is his brother Damien - and a few other peoples - although I don't have their permission to tell you their names."

"Okay," Benji had to accept the verbal boundaries Zarah was setting, but she expected he would be trying to work things out for himself from now on. Indeed, he had gotten this far.

"So our sister had been going out with a hundred-odd year old vampire and shared some kinky love bites with him earlier that day; not long before she got all jealous over Lena and ran off to her death," Zarah said.

"And instead of dying, she became a vampire," Benji said. "Cool!"

"Not so cool," Zarah asserted. "Now Christy will live forever and currently wants to eat her own family. She is also very angry at Eduard because she found out he dated her grandmother before her!"

Benji chuckled. "Christy always was very possessive," he said. "So can't she learn to cope? Eduard goes to school like a normal boy."

"She might learn to cope," Zarah said, "But it will take months or years, that's why we have told Mum and Dad she is at a rehabilitation hospital."

"So where is she really?" Benji asked.

"The Woodgate Estate," Zarah replied.

"I want to see her," Benji cried.

"So do I," Zarah sighed. "But Damien said not tonight."

Benji nodded with wisdom beyond his fourteen-and-a-half years. "Maybe better after the rat hunt. Safer like." His attention wandered back to his homework and his computer. He was only a sophomore after all. "I'll have my sandwich now if it is ready."

Wednesday was a quiet day at school. The major excitement came from a flyer issued by Sheriff Favor announcing that the following day, Thursday, had been selected as the official day for the rat hunt due to the outstandingly bright weather forecast.

All citizens who wished to offer their assistance were to assemble in the town square between the Mystic Evermore Police Station, the Agrarian Council Hall and shopping precinct. They were to wear protective clothing which covered them from wrist to toe, and sturdy boots whenever possible. The Sheriff would be organizing them into hunting parties and Captain Etheridge would be providing some special equipment.

Zarah was relieved the rat hunt would be held soon. The rats were beginning to crawl out of the city drains and gutters and climb into houses, so that one could be found in any dark corner, or long unopened cupboard. Garages and sheds were also full of nasty little nests. The Council exterminators had been called in to eradicate a few infestations, but a city wide effort appeared advisable.

****

The morning of the great rat hunt dawned fine. Many weather forecasts had been studied and barometers consulted when picking the day. Although no one wanted to wait too long before clearing the town of vermin, a clear sunny day would give them an advantage. Even emergency service personnel and community members who were not privy to the true nature of the vampire bats also nodded in acknowledgement of this bit of folk wisdom. It would clearly be much more pleasant going out on a hunt on a nice day.

Zarah reflected there might be some sort of subconscious race-memory buried in the minds of the Mystic Evermore residents as they gathered together so eager to cleanse their community of pests. The hunt had been sanctioned by Sheriff Favor and Mrs. Woodgate as representatives of the law and the Agrarian Council, and when they heard the call the residents had responded almost instinctually.

The Mystic Evermore police effort was being coordinated by Sheriff Favor and Damien Nevermore. On the surface, this appeared to be a strange combination, but the Sheriff did have a habit of conferring emergency deputy powers upon Damien when a crisis occurred. The fire brigade and other emergency service efforts were being commanded by their usual squadron leaders and Captain Etheridge. As Captain Etheridge was in the US Army, no one questioned his right to command.

The civilians were being coordinated by Mrs. Woodgate and Noah Bumble. Mrs. Woodgate was the town Mayor, and her fiancé Noah Bumble was one of Mystic Evermore's respected senior members. While Noah was looking a little old and frail, his son-in-law George Tilton, who managed the Mystic Evermore Recreation Centre, was adding his support for the leg work.

The senior students from the high school had been conscripted to help as a form of community service. The juniors, however, were meant to be attending school and helping with the hunt on the school grounds under the protection of their teachers.

Paul Booth and Zarah Strahan both had notes from their fathers permitting them to contribute to the town efforts, but Benji had gone to school as normal. Benji had suggested Mr. Yore would need all the support he could get in organizing the hunt. While Mr. Yore was very fit and resourceful, many of the female teachers were afraid of the rats, and some of the little children would need defending.

Sheriff Favor grabbed the portable megaphone and began to give instructions. She thanked the citizens for coming and contributing to the effort. Then she emphasized the need for protective gear. It was vitally important to avoid being bitten as Doctors were not sure what viruses these rats might be carrying.

As instructed in the flyer, which had been distributed on Wednesday, all hunt participants were to wear long trousers and long sleeved tops. Hats and gloves were also desirable, and tradesmen who owned steel capped boots were to wear them.

Captain Etheridge then began to speak. He announced that he had a stock of army boots and shin guards that he was about to distribute to community members who did not have their own protective gear. There were also sturdy reinforced gloves that reached almost to the elbow available, and anyone who needed one of these items was to raise their hand. The Captain regretted he did not have enough for every single citizen, so he asked that the most vulnerable members of the hunt receive first preference.

Sheriff Favor took over the megaphone as the protective gear was being distributed. She explained that to avoid unnecessary damage to property, it was desirable that each land-owner lead the hunt on their own land when the hunters arrived. The parties would remain under the control of an experienced squadron leader of course!

The Sheriff then handed the megaphone back to Captain Etheridge who began to distribute more army issue tools. Very few town residents really understood why a silver dipped pitchfork would be more effective than their own garden fork, but they were perfectly happy to line up to collect one. The strong pointy sticks appeared handy and were also accepted happily by the residents.

Each squad leader was given a stock of 'flash bombs' to drop into dark spaces and flush the rats out. No one explained why the light would be more effective than traditional smoke methods of clearing vermin, but everyone accepted the army technology happily. Members of the police force, fire brigade and trained emergency personnel, who could be trusted to manage them had been issued impressive looking flame throwers, with instructions to incinerate rats without burning the town down.

Grandma Strahan crept up beside Zarah. "Will Christy be alright through this?" she whispered.

"We have to hope so," Zarah whispered in reply. "Eduard and Carlice are over there guarding her, and will not leave her side."

"I hope that is enough," Grandma shuddered. "I can't bear the thought of Christy being hunted down like those rats."

"If people obey the rules, the hunt on the Woodgate land will be led by Jaylen, and he will want to keep his cellars secret," Zarah assured her grandmother.

"I hope you are right," Grandma Strahan muttered and then left the assembly area to supervise the hunters when they came to the Strahan General Store. Grandma would be happy to see the end of the rats, but she would tolerate no looting!

The Sheriff and Damien began to assemble people into groups.

Families and people who wanted to hunt together were standing round in clusters, and these were approved with a few adjustments, such as a trained police officer or fire-fighter added to the party to operate the flame throwers and detonate flash-bombs.

Zarah glanced around for anyone she knew from the senior class. They were mostly sorting into groups alongside their parents. She wondered where she and Paul would be assigned, as her father and Wilson had already joined a group of strong men and firefighters. Mum was helping Mrs. Woodgate with the maps at the town hall. Apart from a tendency to treat her mother as a servant, which Barb Strahan wryly tolerated, Mum and Mrs. Woodgate got along quite well.

Damien Nevermore and Sheriff Favor approached the grassy edge where Zarah and Paul were standing. They were accompanied by Javier Tilton and Jaylen Woodgate.

"I want you kids to stick together," Damien said with a wink. "Don't tackle anything that is too hard for you."

"Okay," Paul said.

Sheriff Favor began to object. "They must be accompanied by an adult!"

"Alright," Damien said. "Jamie Lenore will join them whenever he is needed."

"Jamie is merely a glorified junior," Sheriff Favor objected.

Damien glanced around and his eye came to rest on John Booth, who looked pale and thin, but was grasping a silver tipped pitch fork with uncharacteristic determination. It was even unusual for John to have left his house, other than on a domestic errand.

"John can join them," Damien said.

"Oh but," the Sheriff began, but settled down as Damien laid a gentle hand on her arm.

"Sarah, John can go with the children," Damien purred.

The normally strong willed Sheriff melted. "Of course, if you think so," she said.

"I do," Damien almost seemed to sniff John Booth. "There's true Booth in him yet."

"Thank you Damien," John Booth seemed enormously flattered.

"Who will I give the walky-talky and flash bombs to in this group then?" the Sheriff seemed puzzled.

"John, you were an army reserve once, before your accident

weren't you?" Damien said.

John looked surprised anyone remembered. "Yes sir!"

"The boys can carry the gear for you if it is too heavy, but only you may operate the fire-power, do you understand?" Damien announced.

"Oh yes sir," John agreed crisply.

"Very good then," Damien and the Sheriff moved along.

Paul looked concerned. "This is going to take a lot out of you Dad."

John shrugged: "I can help my town in crisis as well as the next man." He glanced defiantly up at the podium where Mrs. Woodgate was surrounded by her pedigreed supporters.

"Let's go," Javier said. "Where have we been assigned?"

"The Strahan General Store, the Woodgate Estate and the strip of land stretching back to Old Mill Farm," John said.

Javier frowned. "Old Mill Farm?"

"You wanted to visit it," Jaylen barked.

"That was then," Javier said. "When I didn't believe."

"We are all believers here, that's why we are together," John said shrewdly. "Lead the way to the store please Zarah."

There were five of them, but they all managed to squeeze into John's battered old station wagon. John did not really need directions to find the Strahan General Store, he shopped there several times a week, and that had been a figure of speech. However, as the family representative, Zarah was technically in charge.

Gran spotted the group as soon as they drew up at the general store. She looked relieved and slightly affronted to have been assigned such a small group, the majority of whom were teen-agers.

"Are you sure you are up to this?" she asked.

Jaylen nodded. "I assure you we are excellent hunters, Grandma Strahan," he said.

Grandma Strahan adjusted her glasses and peered closer. "Jaylen Woodgate - you are the captain of the football team aren't you?"

"Yes, Grandma," Jaylen said. Everyone in Mystic Evermore called Grandma Strahan 'grandma' and Jaylen was not claiming any blood relationship.

"You might be some good for something then after all," Grandma Strahan said. "I don't have any rats that I know of in the shop, some appear in the storage out the back, but most seem to emerge from the waste system."

"Do you mean the big drain Granny?" Zarah asked.

"Okay," John Booth said. "I think Paul and I can clear out the storage rooms. Zarah please take the boys to the big drain. And boys - don't get tempted to use the flash bombs - there could be flammable gasses in the pipes down there."

"Hmm," Zarah said. She wondered what use Javier and Jaylen would be around at the main drain, but she led them around to the rear of the store and indicated the inspection hatch. "In there."

"Lift the lid," Jaylen ordered. "I'm going in."

"It could be smelly," Zarah warned.

"What do you think we are on?" Jaylen exclaimed. "A Sunday picnic?"

Javier levered open the hatch and helped Jaylen drop into the space below. Zarah peered inside. There was space enough for a tradesman to work just below the hatch, but it looked extremely uncomfortable to proceed any further.

"He would have to bend almost double," Zarah complained. "Then how would he fight?"

"Jaylen is very clever isn't he Jaylen?" Javier said. "Jaylen - go."

Zarah had turned to face Javier while he was speaking, so she lost sight of Jaylen for a moment. There was a scuffle and the sound of running footsteps from the main drain. She almost thought she heard a dog barking.

"Where did Jaylen go?" she exclaimed. "Aren't you going to help him?"

"Jaylen is good on his own," Javier said. "I need to make sure he doesn't get locked in down there."

Zarah shuddered. "That would be most unpleasant."

Javier leaned down into the hatch. "Hold my feet please," he said to Zarah. "I don't want to fall in head first."

Zarah caught Javier's legs and leant her weight on them.

"Jaylen," Javier called. "Are you okay down there? How much longer do you need?"

"Rough," echoed back up the drain from Jaylen. "Rough, Rough."

"Okay buddy," Javier called. "Come back as soon as you can - we are worried about you."

A few minutes later, the running footsteps returned to their drain. There was a scuffle and Javier reached towards the rest of the pipe. "Come back Jaylen."

Jaylen crawled out of the drain. He was muddy below the elbows and knees, but otherwise surprisingly clean for someone who had been crawling around in pipes. Zarah had seen her father and Wilson get grubbier. "The pipes go for miles," he said.

Zarah nodded. "My dad laid half of them, and his dad before him, the Strahan's have been plumbers since the founding of Mystic Evermore."

"Do you want to go back inside?" Javier inquired.

Jaylen shook his head. "Not really. I think some of the pipes can be better accessed elsewhere."

Zarah nodded. "Yeah, Dad has some bigger hatches near the mall."

"Well, fancy that, a plumber's eye view of the city," Javier exclaimed.

"That's why Dad is – well Dad!" Zarah explained.

"Interesting," Javier said. "I think I'll stay me."

"Dad already has an apprentice," Zarah said. "Wilson."

"So Wilson Booth is going to be the next guardian of the bowels of the city," Javier remarked.

Zarah giggled. "When you put it like that, it sounds like something from Benji's computer games."

"I'm a gamer myself," Javier said.

"It shows," Zarah replied. Even gaming did not explain Javier's penchant for black coats and other Goth garb, but Zarah did not know him well enough to ask for an explanation. She just assumed it was his taste.

"How secure is it down below Jaylen?" Javier asked. "Can the rats run all the way back here from the city center?"

"Nah bud," Jaylen said. "I replaced one of the big filters that is meant to direct waste down towards the treatment works. Someone had moved it."

"That's odd," Zarah said. She knew her father was very strict about that sort of thing. It contributed to the town's health and safety, as everyone assumed an uncontaminated water supply, and the efficient disposal of storm water and sewerage. "Would a flash bomb have helped down there Jaylen?"

"No, it would have blinded me too," Jaylen said. "Please Zarah, don't go letting off any flash bombs when I'm down in tight spaces."

"Alright," Zarah said.

They replaced the inspection hatch on the main drain and went back into the shop, where they found Paul and John Booth had declared the area 'all clear'.

"Thank you dears," Grandma said. "Would you like soft drinks?"

"Um - we are dirty," Jaylen said.

"We are here to hunt, not snack," John Booth agreed.

However, Grandma insisted and they left carrying sealed screw top bottles. These would stay closed until they were truly thirsty.

"On to the Woodgate Estate," Jaylen instructed John when they were settled into the car. "We will work our way back towards Old Mill Farm from there."

"Don't you think perhaps start at the Old Mill and work our way out to the Estate?" John inquired.

Jaylen laughed his sharp barking laugh. "No," he said. "I happen to know the Estate and the surrounding woods are fairly clean. These rats are worst where there is waste and rubbish from humans."

"Alright if you say so," John agreed. "It sounds like a strategy to me."

It was a good thing they did drive straight to the Woodgate Estate, because when they arrived, they found a bunch of firefighters beating the bushes in the area around the car park.

"What are you doing here?" Jaylen inquired.

"Well, when the Sheriff came to her senses, she decided this area was too dangerous for you kids and sent us out here to help," explained the Squadron Leader, whose name was Ben Vaughn. He was also Anna Vaughn's uncle.

"And she was right," the Second in Command added. "These woods are far too dangerous for kids."

"Alright," Jaylen said. Time was of essence and he wasn't going to argue. "However, this is my land - technically you are under my command."

The firefighters appeared inclined to dissent, so Jaylen repeated: "Upon my father's death, I became the landowner here. The Sheriff specified that you respect the landowner."

"Lead the way then," Squad Leader Ben said. However, he

looked askance at the two juniors and their frail adult chaperone.

Jaylen made a show of looking around the area. "It appears you have cleared here." He marched across to a pile of rocks and tapped them with a loose stone. "Nothing here!" he announced in a loud voice.

Zarah giggled. She suspected that the pile of stones did disguise the cellars where Eduard, Carlice and Christy were hiding. Jaylen was deliberately making a loud noise to give them warning.

One of the firefighters remembered something of the area. "What about the old cellars?" he asked.

"My father had them sealed up - with cement," Jaylen said. He omitted the fact that the sealing had been done on Jaylen's own request and actually made the cellars more habitable.

"There still appears to be something of a crevice here," Squad Leader Ben said, pointing to a dark gap between two rocks.

"Drop a flash-bomb in there," Jaylen commanded. "Nothing will survive within meters of the flash-bomb," he continued in a loud voice.

"There is no need to shout young man," Ben objected, but he did as instructed and commanded his men to drop a flash bomb into the cavity. There was a loud bang, a minimum of smoke and flickers of bright light shone through gaps between the stone. "All cleared."

Zarah was terrified and hid her face in Paul's shoulder.

"Don't worry little girl," a friendly Firefighter said. "Flash bombs aren't radioactive or anything. We are perfectly safe."

"Thank you," Zarah stammered. However, she continued to shake. What if - as she suspected, that was Christy's hiding place - and her sister had not got far enough back in time?

"Don't stress," Jaylen whispered. "They would have gone to the inner cellars."

Zarah needed to know for sure, but there was no way of checking on her sister with the firefighters and other strangers nearby. She just had to harden her heart and bear the worry. The junior thought desperately about her mobile phone, as perhaps she could text Carlice. However, she had been warned that the rocky covering could reduce signal and Carlice might not be able to reply.

Heading the firefighters away from the entrance to the cellars was now Jaylen's main priority, so he gave orders for the area around the river and back towards the boundary to be searched. The far side of the boundary had been assigned to Elisha Blackermore's team, as was the area immediately surrounding Mount Mystic.

The land beyond was wild, rocky and steep, and the towns-people had been relieved when the reclusive millionaire volunteered to search it himself. People muttered it would take a helicopter crew to access the more awkward terrain, but Elisha Blackermore probably had access to such things.

The party reached the boundary of the Woodgate land, where Jaylen ordered them to turn towards town and bear back in the direction of Old Mill Farm. There were several small properties between the Woodgate Estate and old Mill Farm, but they were mostly wooded and appeared healthy. A few nests of rats were found in holes along the creek bed, along with a rabbit or two.

As they approached the Old Mill Farm, however, nests of giant rats became more numerous. The firemen were most efficient at staking and incinerating all they found. Zarah had to admire their technique, it was almost as if they were putting out rats like they usually put out the fires.

Although there were rumors that the Old Mill Farm had been tenanted that year, there were no signs it had been worked. Straggly crops grew in some fields, but they appeared self-seeded, the remnants of kernels dropped when there was a farmer to sow and harvest each year.

The apple trees were over-burdened with fruit, some of which was last seasons and was almost rotting on the tree. The new season's apples were stunted and underdeveloped because the trees had not been tended or pruned recently.

A few pigs roamed the property. These had escaped their pens and become free-range, and their offspring were almost wild. Even domestic pigs can bite, so the hunters took care not to approach the wild pigs. Several of the firemen had the idea of herding them back into their old yards, and were using the stakes as sticks and making loud noises to encourage them in the correct direction.

Paul and John Booth were looking thoughtful and passing their hands over the backs of the penned pigs from a safe distance. One or two they pronounced clean, but they ordered the firemen to incinerate the rest, because they pronounced them to be 'infected'. The firemen looked puzzled, but the plague-ridden pigs smelt so foul and unlike normal farm pigs that they obeyed.

"Surely they are not vampire pigs?" Zarah whispered to Paul.

Paul shook his head. "Not yet," he whispered. "But someone appears to be attempting to hybridize them."

"Like the rats?" Zarah inquired.

"Somewhat similar to the rats," Paul said. "Dad and I can sense the rotting cells."

The farm kitchen appeared to have been used recently, although not for cooking a meal fit for human consumption. Some meat, perhaps from a pig, had been chopped on the benchtop. There was no evidence that it had been cooked, rather it appeared to have been eaten raw.

Perhaps, Zarah speculated, the meat had been thrown back to the other pigs, who appeared quite capable of being cannibals. There was very little furniture in the farmhouse, and no one was around.

The party turned their attention to the old mill silo. This had stairs leading to the top, where an area had been converted into an almost cozy looking resting place. A hatch near the bottom, however, opened into a darkened vault, from where an awful smell arose.

Some of the firemen, hardened emergency service personnel though they were, refused to enter the tomb-like base of the silo. They volunteered to keep searching the property and destroying infected pigs, and the squadron leader let them go.

"Everyone has their strengths," Ben explained to Zarah. "Some of the guys have no fear of heights, and yet dislike confined spaces. They are all good men in an emergency."

Zarah nodded. She could understand even brave men had their fears.

John and Paul turned to Jaylen and Javier. "I'm afraid we do have to go in there," John said. "The scent of evil is very strong."

"I know," Jaylen looked pale. "Javier - I'll go ahead."

There was a series of soft thumps and Jamie Lenore joined the group. He appeared to have been running to catch up with them, but had hardly broken a sweat. He was breathing quickly, but not panting. He carried a barbaric looking crossbow with silver tipped arrows and his muscles rippled all along his arms. He appeared to have torn his shirt in a number of places.

"Wait for me," Jamie said. He glanced around at the party.

"Didn't Damien say I would join you when I was needed?"

"All right bud," Javier said. "Go for it."

Jaylen and Jamie disappeared into the black hole. A few seconds later, Javier indicated the rest of the party ought to enter. Jamie was waiting inside, poking around in some rubbish, but Jaylen was nowhere to be seen. Instead a massive grey timber wolf was digging a hole, clearing the entrance to some sort of tunnel.

"Don't hurt the dog," Jamie said. "He's helping."

The remaining firemen traced crosses in the air in a superstitious manner.

"That ain't no dog," Squad Leader Ben exclaimed. "It's a ruddy great wolf. Bigger than we normally get in these parts too!"

"It's my pet," Javier said. "Just be glad it's on our side."

"I'd heard you had a big dog, Master Tilton," Ben said. "You brought some mighty strange ideas out here from Chicago where you came."

"Huh?" Javier made meaningless noise. It was better to be thought eccentric than have his secrets exposed. "Maybe strange to you."

The wolf had finished uncovering the depression in the side of the silo, revealing a sloping tunnel that led some distance into the ground. The smell from the hole was even worse if possible. A slithering scuffling sound rose faintly from deeper underground.

"I'm going in," Jamie said. "Javier, look after Zarah. Paul, I may need your help."

"We are all coming of course," Zarah said, as she followed the boys. The tunnel gave her the creeps, but she was not risking losing Paul either. She was also determined to do her bit even if all she could do was spear something with a stake.

They stumbled along for some distance, the shadows barely pierced by the large torches carried by the fireman. Rats that scuttled around corners were neatly crunched in the jaws of the huge wolf. Zarah was relieved to notice that the rats appeared to break into dust and were not ingested by the wolf. If the wolf was Jaylen, as she somehow suspected, it would be unbearable to think of his actually eating the vampire rats. Fresh game maybe, but vampire rats - never.

The tunnel seemed to widen out into a cave that contained the most curious round tank like a vat. A squat creature floated in the vat. It had a bulbous body and three deformed heads, each of which glowed an eerie luminous green.

"Someone has been trying to play god," Jamie remarked. He pulled his bow back, and firing in rapid succession, pin-cushioned the creature with silver arrows.

The creature writhed in pain, but did not die. The wolf took one of the creature's six arms in its huge jaws and began to pull. Two firemen stepped forward and emptied the tanks of their flame throwers into the amorphous blob that formed the creature's nether regions.

Finally, it seemed to shrivel and die. Unlike the vampire rats, which turned to dust, this creature left a pile of slime in the tank.

"What did you mean?" Zarah asked Jamie. "Playing god?"

"I think he meant trying to create life using primordial slime," Javier explained.

"What he said," Jamie returned. "But not so technical." Now that the monster was dead, he seemed restless, the hunter in him seeking its next quarry.

A creaking sound, so slight that the group almost missed hearing it, heralded the opening of some sort of flap. Then there was the more audible thud of a lid or trapdoor.

"Who is there?" a voice that may have once been human whispered.

"Show yourself," Jamie ordered.

"I'm too smart for that," the undead whisper rang around the room, seeming to come from all directions.

"We have killed your creature," Javier added persuasively. "Come out and we will talk."

Javier was using a tone he had never used in her hearing before. Zarah found his voice soothing and attractive. If she had been an animal, she would have gone to him. The wolf stuck close by his side.

The unnatural creature also seemed drawn to Javier's voice. It appeared in the outer beams of the firefighter's torch light. It had once been a beautiful woman, but was now thin and haggard. It was wearing a rich gown and hood, that had become bedraggled in the dust of the hole. The skin glowed deathly pale in the torchlight, and the eyes were strangely compelling. Two large teeth protruded either side of its mouth.

"I am Henrietta Ermore," the creature spoke. "I have been here since the town began. All those who follow my ways are my children."

"The mother of all evil," Jamie muttered. "At least for this region. Let me at her!"

Javier raised a restraining hand. "Wait just a minute," he instructed Jamie. "If you should die," he asked Henrietta, "Would all the other Mystic Evermore vampires die too?"

"I don't know," Henrietta replied. "Those who have lost all vestige of their humanity might die."

"Interesting," Javier said.

"Does it matter?" Jamie cried, full of the blood-lust and instinctual need to hunt. "They are evil leeches!"

"It might according to Captain Etheridge's new rules," Javier said. "Anyone who can be redeemed must be given a second chance. What about the younger vampires?"

Zarah gave a great cry and clutched at her chest. She could not bear it if killing this creature, which literally emanated evil, also destroyed her sister. It was an age old conundrum, something like the one involving free will, and the question regarding whether evil ought to be allowed to exist, simply to empower freedom of choice?

Henrietta Ermore laughed a screeching laugh. "Your so-called young vampires, are so barely stepped into the darkness so as to be partially human still. If they have made many kills, they will be weakened when I die. If they have saved lives as well as damned them, they may live along with you human scum."

"I think she has made her position fairly clear," Jamie said.

Javier was not finished however. "We have hunted many vampire rats today," he said. "Were the vampire rats your creations too?"

"The rats?" Henrietta the Vampiress moaned. "Oh my lovelies." The Vampiress beckoned, and one of the firemen was entranced. He began to approach her. The squadron leader and John Booth together pulled the fireman back into line.

"Don't go to her," John said. "If she gets fresh blood, she will be strengthened."

"I smell a Booth," the Vampiress said, her head swiveling towards John. "You... I seem to remember you!"

"I bound you once before," John exclaimed. "It has taken you almost twenty years to wake again."

"Binding me drained your power," the Vampiress snarled. "You could not overcome me again."

"But perhaps I could," Paul said stepping into the torchlight. "And together Dad and I could destroy you."

The Vampiress turned to face him. "Fresh Booth," she said. "Smells untrained. I could drain you too."

Henrietta began to levitate and swayed towards the more vulnerable human members of the attack party. The wolf instinctively rose from its crouch behind Javier and leapt towards the Vampiress, tearing viciously into her throat. The Mater Vampire raised a bony arm and tossed the wolf aside. He fell onto the compacted dirt with a thud, obviously injured, but clutching a scrap of her dress determinedly in his jaws.

Jamie Lenore let loose an arrow, piercing the Vampiress through the side. As if they had been awaiting the signal to attack, two firemen ran forward with stakes. They were obviously regretting having used all the flame thrower fuel on the three headed monster, but still determined to do their bit.

Paul and John Booth joined hands and began to chant, small balls of fire emerging from their cupped hands and streaming towards the Vampiress. The combination of attacks distressed the Vampiress and she began to wail. Losing control of her levitation, she too crumpled to the floor and lay within inches of the wolf.

Jamie stepped forward, and drawing an axe out of his belt, chopped off her head. Minutes later, there was nothing left other than a pile of dust.

"Let's get out of here," Jamie suggested. "I expect she was the nurturer of the rat plague and we will have no more troubles for some time."

"Help me with my dog," Javier cried, struggling to lift the great wolf by himself.

"Is the wolf dead?" Paul asked.

"Hopefully only stunned," Jamie said, helping Javier carry the wolf towards the entrance.

Once Javier and Jamie reached the sweet grass outside, they laid the wolf's body carefully down. Javier cradled the wolf's head on his lap and shielded it from view with his body.

When Javier rose from his crouch and faced the men, the wolf was no longer to be seen on the ground behind Javier. Instead, Jaylen

Woodgate appeared from around the side of the silo. He was holding his side, which appeared to be badly bruised.

"You are hurt, Master Woodgate," Ben, the leader of the firemen, exclaimed in concern.

"It is nothing," Jaylen said. "I will heal."

"Whatever happened in the silo?" the dazed Firefighters asked in confusion. "Did we really kill a three headed monster? Was that woman the ghost of Old Mill Farm? And did John and Paul Booth actually throw fire from their hands?"

Javier raised a reassuring hand. "You were in a fight, it was dark and confusing," he said in his most charismatic voice. "You were very brave. The Booths had miniature flash bombs supplied by Captain Etheridge."

Squadron Leader Ben nodded solemnly. "That could be - dark - confusing - flash bombs. We must go back to headquarters and make our report at once."

****

Zarah barely slept all Thursday night because she was consumed with anxiety about Christy. She was happy that the evil Mater Vampire, Henrietta Ermore, who had created countless other vampires, mutants and hybrid creatures, had been destroyed. However, despite Henrietta's assertion that the younger vampires, and those who had maintained their humanity, Zarah had read too many stories where the entire line of supernatural creatures was wiped out upon the death of their forebear.

Zarah had tried texting Carlice several times and Carlice had not answered. Of course, Carlice was buried under a rock pile which could be muffling the signal. Moreover, mobiles can go flat. It was hard to imagine in the technological era, but Zarah had learned that a person did not cease to exist just because their mobile sat unanswered.

Zarah showered and dressed and got ready for school because it was expected of her. Their mother drove Zarah and Benji to school early, in the hope the teens would visit the library and do some study to make up for classes that had been disrupted the previous day. Once at school, Zarah glanced around, hoping she might see Carlice or Eduard. However, neither appeared to be at school.

Zarah approached Ivy Pinkerton at recess time for information about the senior class. Ivy did not know where Carlice and Eduard might be, but she reported that Jaylen had a cracked rib which was discretely strapped to his side. Ivy also suggested that Lena Lenore might know something because she went way back with the Nevermore brothers, having dated Eduard at one time, and even Damien briefly as rumor might have it.

Lena was leaning against her locker, talking to Javier Tilton. The brunette, who was one of the most popular girls in school, straightened and viewed Zarah with an air of superiority. "What do you want Eduard and Carlice for?" she asked.

"I just want to find out if they are alright," Zarah said.

"That's sweet of you," Lena said. "But Eduard and I haven't been talking lately."

"I know I heard," Zarah stammered. It was awkward with her sister Christy having formed the third point of the love triangle between Eduard and Lena. "I just thought you might have seen them."

"Carlice is still my friend," Lena said thoughtfully. "Are you saying she is really missing?"

"I don't really know," Zarah stammered. "She won't answer her mobile telephone."

"Probably screening her calls against juniors," Lena remarked somewhat unkindly, although this was exactly the sort of thing Carice might have done in the days when she was the most popular girl in the school.

"Why don't you try Bridget Etheridge?" Javier suggested more generously. "She doesn't appear to be here either."

"Good idea," Zarah said. She dialed Bridget's number herself because she happened to have it saved amongst her contacts.

A tired sounding voice answered. "Bridget here."

"Oh Didge!" Zarah exclaimed in relief. "Where are you and have you seen Eduard and Carlice?"

"I'm at the Nevermore Manor," Bridget replied. "Damien is sick. I haven't seen Eduard or Carlice today."

"Damien is sick?" Zarah was alarmed. It sounded as though a malady had indeed struck their vampire friends.

"Yeah, he collapsed suddenly yesterday, towards the end of the rat hunt," Bridget said. "Daddy took him back to the Manor and put him to bed - for a while there - we though he was going to die."

"Oh no," Zarah exclaimed.

"Towards morning, Damien was burning up with fever and muttering about his burden of guilt. Daddy even gave him the tiniest shot of this experimental drug he is working on, although he warned it was nowhere ready to be used," Bridget explained.

"Did it help any?" Zarah was breathless.

"Damien is sleeping now and it looks as though he might be alright," Bridget murmured. "What was that you were saying about Eduard and Carlice?"

"No one has seen or heard from them since the day before yesterday," Zarah said. "They were meant to have been down the cellars at the Woodgate Estate."

"I'll send Daddy over to have a look," Bridget offered. "The Sheriff is here trying to hold Damien's hand as well, so we are well chaperoned, especially for a couple who have broken up."

"Perhaps your father ought not to go there alone," Zarah suggested nervously. "Even army heroes need buddies."

"Of course," Bridget said. "He will drop by the school and collect Jaylen. I doubt he could find the cellar entrance without assistance. Especially if Jaylen covered it up for any reason."

About half an hour later, Captain Etheridge arrived at Mystic Evermore High and requested an interview with Jaylen Woodgate. A few minutes later, he signed Jaylen out from school and they set off towards the Woodgate Estate. Zarah spied them going out of the gate and begged to be allowed to go along with them.

At first Captain Etheridge said, "No," but after a significant nod from Jaylen he changed his mind and said, "Yes."

Then there were more leave forms to complete, and Zarah's grandmother had to be called for permission. Zarah had picked her grandmother to ask for permission because she thought that Grandma Strahan would understand and give permission easily. However, Grandmother insisted in being allowed to come along as well.

Grandma discretely put Zarah's mother in charge of the store, and was waiting out the front when Captain Etheridge drove through town. The rescue party then drove across the northern bridge to the Woodgate Estate, where Captain Etheridge dew to a halt in the cleared circle that served as a parking area.

"You women stay in the car," Captain Etheridge said sternly to Zarah and Grandma Strahan, before asking Jaylen to show him the correct stones to move. "I wouldn't want to cause a cave-in," he remarked.

"Over here sir," Jaylen said, picking his way through the rubble toward the tree line. The strong boy and fit man worked fervently for some time clearing the entrance.

"You really did not mean anyone to uncover the tunnels yesterday did you?" Captain Etheridge said wryly to Jaylen. "Whatever were you hiding?"

"A new vampire unfortunately sir," Jaylen returned. "You heard about Christy Strahan's accident last weekend?"

"I had also heard she was safely in a rehabilitation facility undergoing physiotherapy," Captain Etheridge observed ruefully. "It goes to show you shouldn't believe anything you hear around this town."

"Probably not sir," Jaylen agreed cynically.

Zarah peered out of the car window in excitement. "Are you going down there now?"

"Yes," Captain Etheridge replied. "Please wait patiently Zarah, we really don't know what we will find."

It seemed like an eternity, but was really only a little while before Captain Etheridge and Jaylen appeared, carrying a bundle that looked like a body wrapped securely in blankets. They placed it in the trunk of the vehicle and shut the lid.

"What's that?" Zarah cried in alarm.

"It's Eduard," Captain Etheridge explained. "He is in a bad way. I will take him back to Nevermore Manor and see what I can do for him."

"Oh no," Grandma Strahan moaned. "Oh poor Edward." "Why not hospital?" Zarah asked.

Captain Etheridge shook his head. "Hospitals are no good for vampires."

Grandmother Strahan appeared torn between her responsibilities as Zarah and Christy's grandmother and the lover of her youth. Duty however won: "What about young Carlice and Christy?" she asked.

"Please say they are okay?" Zarah begged.

"They are both young vampires," Captain Etheridge said. "They appear to be better off than Eduard and should recover fully."

"Can I go and see my sister?" Zarah asked.

"I will be accompanying Zarah," Grandma Strahan announced firmly.

Captain Etheridge nodded. "Jaylen will take you downstairs. I'm sorry to leave you alone here, but Mrs. Strahan will be in charge until I get back."

"Very good captain," Grandma Strahan agreed. "How exactly are the girls?"

"Christy is sleepy and confused and not capable of eating anyone at the moment!" Captain Etheridge announced. "Carlice is even more sluggish, and she has always had the control required to attend school as a normal girl. There is no risk to either of you."

"That's not what she meant," Zarah exclaimed indignantly, but Jaylen tugged at her arm impatiently.

"Come on," Jaylen said. "Let me take you downstairs and you will see for yourselves. The sooner Captain Etheridge gets Eduard back to Nevermore Manor the better."

"I do hope dear Edward will recover," Grandmother Strahan murmured, but she allowed herself to be led towards the cellar entrance and down the steps. "This is quite impressive young man. I didn't know there was so much of the old building left."

"I had a few discrete repairs done," Jaylen admitted.

"It's dark," Zarah complained. There was little light beside the small pool thrown by the torch Captain Etheridge had given Grandma Strahan to hold.

"No electricity," Jaylen admitted. "I don't usually need it."

At the bottom of the stairs was an area Jaylen had furnished in a rough manner for when he was camping out. Zarah had to admit it was remarkable so far as camp-sites went.

Beyond Jaylen's normal campsite was an inner cellar whose entrance was blocked with steel bars. Zarah gave a cry of horror, but Jaylen shrugged.

"Sometimes I do need security," Jaylen said. He touched some of the steel bars and they swung aside, apparently they were set into a door.

Inside the inner chamber, Christy and Carlice were lying on rocky shelves, which had been padded for comfort using sleeping bags and blankets.

"Christy," Grandma Strahan cried and swept Christy up into her arms. "How are you feeling?"

Christy returned her grandmother's hug enthusiastically. "I feel like I've got a huge hangover," she said. "However, it is also good to be able to hug my grandmother without being overcome by the urge to snack on her neck."

Zarah spread her arms wide: "Hug me too sis!"

Jaylen approached Carlice. "How are you Car?" he asked. "Even though we are broken up, I don't want to lose you."

"I feel like I have ten hangovers," Carlice replied. "What happened?"

"We found and killed the Mater Vampire, Henrietta Ermore," Jaylen replied.

"Wouldn't that destroy us descendant vampires?" Carlice murmured.

"Javier weighed the risks and found them acceptable," Jaylen explained. "Apparently if you have enough humanity left in you - you will survive."

"It's like judgement day for the lich population of Mystic Evermore area then," Carlice murmured. "Any vampire who has completely lost their humanity will die."

"At least if they have been sired by Henrietta Ermore," Jaylen agreed.

Carlice laughed a bitter little laugh. "It's weird to talk about the death of my own kind, but we should have far less trouble with rogue vampires for a while."

"Not many get past Damien Nevermore and Captain Etheridge, but yeah," Jaylen said.

"Speaking of Damien - how is he?" Carlice inquired. "He is the darkest vampire I know personally."

"Bridget said he was very sick," Zarah informed Carlice. "But the Captain gave him some sort of cure and he will recover."

"Eduard didn't look too good either," Christy observed.

"The Captain took Eduard back to Nevermore Manor for treatment," Jaylen said. "I must admit, he looked pretty bad."

"Poor Edward," Grandma Strahan murmured. "I want to go to him. But first, we must decide what to do about you girls. Would you prefer to come back to the room above the shop, or go to

Nevermore Manor?"

Christy looked a little scared. "It's still light outside," she said. "I don't have one of those magic rings that allows me to survive sunlight yet. Eduard said he had to find a witch willing to manufacture one for me."

"I know you might not want to hear this, Granny Strahan," Carlice said. "But Christy really is safest here!"

"The walls might be a bit bare," Jaylen said, "But other than that - Woodgate Estate is a fine place."

"The woods are very beautiful," Grandma Strahan agreed. "It's just I'm afraid of..."

"All the vampires and werewolves!" Christy said and began to giggle hysterically. "Say if you killed the Mater Vampire - is there a chance I'm human again?"

"If you were human, I think you would be dead," Jaylen observed. "Having fallen on your head in the river and all that!"

Carlice offered Christy a thermos filled with a mysterious dark liquid. "Do you want any of that?"

"Yeah," Christy admitted.

"You're still a vampire then," Carlice said. "Maybe the aggressive instincts are temporarily deadened - but you will have to deal with them again sometime."

"I have been thinking," Christy said. "I need some time to get used to all this. When I'm feeling better I would like to visit that friend you were telling me about Carlice. The one that helped Eduard overcome his violent streak and develop the control required to attend school like a normal boy."

"It would be a good idea," Carlice said. "You could stay with her for a while and come back to Mystic Evermore when you were ready."

"Grandmother, Zarah would you explain to Mum and Dad please?" Christy begged. "Say I will be in rehab a while longer."

"I think they already expect you to be in rehab for some months," Grandmother Strahan said. "Anyone who heard about the severity of your injuries would expect you to be institutionalized for some time. However, I expect your parents would like to receive a phone call when you feel ready."

"Me and Benji too," Zarah said. "We like to hear my big sister's voice occasionally. Please keep in contact!"

Heavy boots sounded on the stairs and Captain Etheridge strode into view carrying another torch. "I hate to break up the party, but visiting time is over ladies," he said.

Grandmother Strahan rose to her feet. "I'm ready," she said. "I would like to stop by Nevermore Manor, Captain."

"That suits," Captain Etheridge said. "My business there is not finished."

Zarah and Grandma gave Christy one more hug and kiss, and then turned and walked along the stone corridor and up the steps.

"I don't know when we will see Christy again," Grandma said. There were tears in her eyes.

"We will have to see what happens," Zarah said. "No one could have predicted what has happened so far."

They closed the wooden trapdoor at the top of the cellar steps and Jaylen scattered a few rocks around to disguise the passage. Then they climbed into the Captain's vehicle and drove towards Nevermore Manor.

Grandma Strahan had her hands clasped tightly and seemed to be praying. Zarah glanced at her curiously. This thing with Eduard Nevermore appeared to run deep for something Grandma had forgotten for over fifty years.

When they reached Nevermore Manor, Damien was sitting in a large reclining chair being fed a funny colored chicken soup by Sheriff Favor, who was all concern and blushes. Eduard however, was lying in bed, almost as dead as the day he had really died.

Bridget Etheridge was keeping vigil by his side, even though her heart was with Damien in the other room.

"Not even a moan or a fever," Bridget whispered.

"Eduard is much worse than Damien ever was," Captain Etheridge pronounced. "He must have lost more of his humanity over the years."

"What do you mean?" Bridget asked in surprise. "Eduard who goes to school with us like a normal boy - and only drinks packaged blood, never fresh blood - is darker than Damien - whom everybody knows has been evil?"

"He must be darker and have saved less lives or he would not be sicker than Damien," Captain Etheridge pronounced. "Appearances can be deceiving."

"Man looketh upon the outer appearance, but the Lord looketh on the heart," Grandma Strahan quoted from somewhere, perhaps the Bible. "Nevertheless, he is my Edward." She seated herself at Eduard's side and took his hand. "You may go back to your own lover girl," she said to Bridget.

"I'm happy to return to Damien," Bridget said, relinquishing her post at Eduard's side. "But is this really the time to be territorial Grandmother Strahan?"

Bridget did not express any surprise at Grandma's declarations of affection towards Eduard, as she was well aware both the Nevermore brothers were over a hundred years old. Both boys were trapped in eternal youth, as their bodies remained roughly the age they had been when they first died.

"I was thinking," Bridget continued practically, "Maybe we should contact Lena Lenore."

"But they aren't even speaking," Zarah exclaimed. "And Eduard moved on with my sister!"

"According to my class-mates," Bridget said, "I admit this was a little before I arrived in Mystic Evermore - Lena and Eduard were once very serious. If Eduard is really dying, I think Lena would want to know."

"Good idea," Captain Etheridge exclaimed. "We will see if Lena can call to the humanity in Eduard. At this point in time, I'm afraid to give him even the tiniest bit of the cure in case his body can't take it."

"She is not my best friend or anything," Bridget said, "But I think I do have Lena's number in my mobile, because she is my classmate."

"If you don't," Captain Etheridge said. "Sheriff Favor would be able to help us."

Thus it was agreed Lena should be called, and when Lena expressed herself willing to come over to Nevermore Manor, Jaylen was sent out to pick her up. He set off driving Captain Etheridge's car and returned some thirty-five minutes later with both Lena and Jamie Lenore. The Lenore cousins climbed out of the car and inquired after the health of the Nevermore brothers.

"Despite my instinctive urge to kill them, I consider Damien and Edward to be among my best friends," Jamie explained paradoxically. He followed Captain Etheridge into the living area and greeted

Damien. "How are you mate?"

"I'm being fussed to death by Sarah and Bridget," Damien said. "I'm so glad you have arrived to rescue me."

"I bet you are loving every minute of it," Jamie pronounced.

Damien smiled his wicked charming smile. "Guilty as charged," he said. "Do sit down."

Lena Lenore continued following Captain Etheridge up the stairs, into the family rooms, and right into Eduard's bedroom. She looked mildly annoyed to see Zarah and Grandmother Strahan, especially as Grandmother Strahan was holding Eduard's hand in a most un-grandmotherly way.

Lena sat down on the opposite side of the bed to Grandmother Strahan and took Eduard's other hand.

"How is he?" Lena asked.

"Pretty bad so far as I can tell," Grandmother Strahan said. "You know what he is - don't you?"

"Of course," Lena said. "I'm not surprised to find he has a past." She leaned down towards Eduard so that her hair brushed the sheet and her lips almost brushed his lips. "Eduard my love."

"Fifty years ago he was known as Edward," Grandma Strahan said with somewhat misty eyes.

"Times change," Lena said. "I'm not threatened by old girlfriends - especially when they have become the town grandmother." That was Lena Lenore as usual treading the fine line between nice and nasty. "Eduard darling - wake up."

Eduard began to toss and turn uncomfortably.

"He has a fever," Lena cried accusingly. "Captain Etheridge, why haven't you done anything about it?"

"Believe me my dear," the Captain displayed infinite patience with the distraught young lover, "Even a fever is an improvement to how he was. Now maybe he could take a little of the cure."

"What cure?" Lena exclaimed.

"It's not perfected," Captain Etheridge explained. "It will just restore the tiniest bit of his humanity, but it might be enough to give him a fighting chance."

"Do it," Lena cried. "Oh Eduard, I cannot lose you."

Captain Etheridge pursed his lips and stepped forward with the syringe. It was a solemn moment. "This worked for Damien," he said. He slid Eduard's shirt down over his shoulder to reveal his upper arm and jabbed carefully.

Eduard thrashed momentarily and then began to calm. He began to mutter and sweat.

"What is happening?" Lena cried.

"Is the cure working?" Grandmother Strahan asked.

"I can't be sure," Captain Etheridge said. "I think the fever is breaking."

Grandmother Strahan picked up a damp cloth and began to sponge Eduard's forehead. "This will bring his temperature down."

"Oh Eduard," Lena murmured. "I do still love you. I know we were on a break - but if you hadn't moved on with Christy we most likely would have got back together."

Eduard opened his eyes. "Am I hallucinating?" he whispered.

"No darling," Lena said. "You have been very sick, but you will get better now."

"Is that really you Lena?" Eduard asked.

"Yes dear," Lena whispered.

"I love you too," Eduard said. "I always did and I always will. It just got too hard when you didn't seem to know your own mind."

"That's over dear," Lena whispered. "Can't we get back together?"

"I think we better leave the lovebirds to it," Captain Etheridge said. He led Zarah and Grandmother Strahan down to the living room. "It looks as though Eduard may survive."

"Good," Damien said. "I wouldn't want to be the only Nevermore brother left."

Zarah realized she was slightly bored. Everyone except for herself and possibly Jaylen, appeared to be highly involved with the Nevermore family, but she had no real connection. She was also getting tired as it had been quite a few hours. Moreover, no one had thought about feeding her, because she had not been one of the victims. Her mobile phone was buzzing. Zarah picked it up.

"Hello Dad," Zarah said.

"Wherever are you Zarah?" Robbie Strahan exclaimed. "I went by the school to pick you up and they told me you had left early."

"I'm at Nevermore Manor," Zarah replied.

"Whatever are you doing there?" Robbie Strahan asked.

"Eduard and Damien were sick. Grandma was helping," Zarah explained.

"Your grandmother is a very kind lady," Robbie said. "But I hope you are not getting any ideas about the Nevermore boys."

"No Dad," Zarah said. "I would be quite happy to be home with you and Mum and Benji. And when it comes to boys, I much prefer Paul Booth! It's just that we arrived in Captain Etheridge's car and there isn't a spare vehicle here to take us home."

"I'll be over to pick you up in a few," Robbie Strahan said. "See if your grandmother is ready to come along too."

****

Saturday morning Zarah opened a sleepy eye, noticed that it was still early, rolled over and went to sleep again. The previous week had been emotionally draining. Her sister had died - but no - she had been transformed into a vampire instead of staying dead. It all seemed like a dream and she ought to hear Christy's voice soon, berating her for being so lazy on a Saturday morning.

An hour later Zarah rolled over again, nothing had changed, Christy was still dead, and the voice calling belonged to her younger brother Benji.

"Yeah," she muttered sleepily.

"Your mobile phone has been ringing," Benji said. "It's Paul Booth. He wants to know why you left school yesterday."

"What are you doing answering my mobile?" Zarah muttered sleepily.

"You left it in the lounge last night," Benji said.

"I was tired," Zarah said. "It's been a big week - Christy and all that."

"I know," Benji said. "I've been feeling like the proverbial excrement too."

"I'm sorry little bro," Zarah said. "Tell Paul to ride his bike over later - we can hang out."

"Are you going to let me hang with you too?" Benji asked.

"I'll think about it," Zarah said. "We kinda like being alone."

"Zarah and Paul sitting in a tree: K-I-S-S-I-N-G," Benji began to chant.

"Yeah we do," Zarah said. "But I'll deny it when I'm properly awake."

"Of course," Benji laughed.

Paul Booth arrived at the Strahan house just after lunch. By that time, Zarah was awake, showered, dressed in smart casual and fed. She was also sitting on the front porch wondering where her friend had got to, when he rode up on his bicycle. Paul dismounted, opened the gate and pushed his bike the last few meters up the driveway.

"The way Benji described you this morning, I thought I'd better give you some time," Paul laughed when Zarah greeted him.

"Oh right," Zarah said. "Um - Benji wants to hang out with us this afternoon - is that okay?"

Paul looked momentarily disappointed. "Sure."

"It's not that I don't want to be alone with you," Zarah said. "He's just my brother and I can't ignore him all the time."

"Yeah," Paul was easily reassured. "What did you want to do?"

"I thought we could ride our bikes over to the Blackermore Estate," Zarah said. "According to Carlice, no one has heard from Elisha Blackermore since the day of the rat hunt. That was Thursday! He was meant to report in with Sheriff Favor about the hunt effort on his own lands and the slopes of Mount Mystic."

"The Blackermores are far older vampires than the Nevermores," Paul said. "If Damien and Eduard got sick - what might have happened to Elisha and Rachel?"

"Indeed," Zarah said.

"But what will we say of we are caught trespassing on the Blackermore Estate?" Paul asked.

"We will say we have business there," Zarah said. "But we won't get caught, no one goes there during the day on the weekend."

"What will we tell Benji?" Paul asked.

"The truth as it arises," Zarah said. "He is a smart kid, he already worked out a lot about Christy."

"Okay," Paul said.

Zarah went inside. "Benz are you ready? We are going for a ride."

Benji looked up from his computer, a bright smile lighting his face. He saved his game and shut down the machine. "Wow thanks for asking me."

"Guilt got to me, don't expect it all the time," Zarah muttered.

Benji and Zarah opened the garage to retrieve their bikes and then joined Paul in the driveway. Zarah opened the gate so they could pass through, and then closed it again. It was a nuisance, but the family had somehow agreed they were more comfortable at home with the gate shut. It had been a development since Christy's accident that showed the family's general withdrawal into grief.

The morning had been cloudy, but the afternoon was proving to be sunny. It was a beautiful day and Zarah found herself humming under her breath as she rode along. They turned north and exited the suburbs, passing the cemetery and then the Farmer's Market. The Old Mill Farm brooded in the sunlight, somehow seeming clearer and less haunted than it had ever been in Zarah's memory. Then they rode past the woodlands until they reached the Woodgate Estate. Zarah was tiring by this time, and had to work hard to pedal the remaining distance past the Woodgate Estate to the Blackermore Estate.

Zarah, Benji and Paul had never been to the Blackermore Estate, although they had driven past with their parents to Mount Mystic several times. They turned in through the impressive gates and rode up the long driveway, past thriving gardens, towards the house. The Blackermore's had employed share-farmers and other contractors, although none of the staff ever lived on the estate, and consequently the grounds were delightfully maintained.

The gardens surrounding the house itself proved to be breathtaking. They were Japanese in style, featuring a pond and fountain, surrounded by bamboo trees and blossoming Japanese fruit trees. Zarah jumped off her bike and hid it amongst some bamboo plants. Paul and Benji did likewise.

"The gardens are beautiful," Zarah breathed.

"Who would have thought," Paul said. "It takes a soul to really appreciate natural beauty."

"I wouldn't like to be here at night though," Zarah said pointing to a pair of statues that stood beside the fountain, facing each other for all the world as if they were talking. "Those statues would be spooky."

"One looks just like Rachel Blackermore," Benji said. "I've seen pictures of her in old albums."

"The other looks a lot like Elisha Blackermore," Paul observed.

"It makes sense," Zarah said. "This is their place, they might have had statues of themselves made."

The teenagers climbed up the stairs and approached the front door. None of them had any idea what they would do should the door prove to be locked, but it wasn't. It swung open under Paul's hand.

"Let me go in first," Paul said. He was the eldest of the boys and had some witchy powers in addition to protect them with.

"Okay," Zarah breathed, but she caught his hand and tagged along close behind Paul.

"Technically we are not breaking and entering," Benji observed. "The place isn't locked."

"Thanks for that Benz," Zarah breathed. "So I'm not risking going to jail, even though I am risking being eaten by vampires."

"Respectable vampires," Paul said. "According to Booth family legends, the Blackermore family have controlled rogue vampires around Mystic Evermore for generations."

"Does that make them good?" Zarah inquired.

"It makes them territorial," Benji observed. "Animals patrol their territory instinctively."

"I'm not sure whether the Blackermores really cared about good or bad," Paul said. "They liked a comfortable life. Violence between vamps and humans disrupted that comfort. That's why we can't be certain what might have happened to them with the death of their Mater."

The teenagers passed through the house, opening the doors to many rooms. All were beautifully furnished with priceless antiques, but none were occupied. The teenagers shivered as they climbed down the stairs to the cellars where the vampires would have had their day-beds, but that area too proved empty.

"Not even a pile of dust," Zarah observed, peering into the satin-lined casket Rachel had preferred. Elisha's was lined with more masculine bear skins and fur. "You would think that if they died when the Mater did, they would leave some dust behind."

"Perhaps they completely disintegrated," Benji suggested. "Is that possible?"

"I don't know - could be," Paul said. "Let's try the sheds and storehouses out the back."

The farm buildings told the same story. They were beautifully stocked and maintained, waiting the return of the contractors on

Monday. However, there was no sign of their resident owners, Rachel and Elisha Blackermore. The teenagers circled around the yards twice to make sure they had checked everywhere.

"Could they have gone out?" Benji suggested at last.

Paul shook his head. "The limousine is in the garage," he said. "Even the helicopter is parked on its pad."

"I'm tired and my feet hurt," Zarah said. "I'm going to paddle in the fountain."

"It doesn't seem right," Paul began.

"I don't care," Zarah said. "There is no one and nothing here except for the two spooky statues." She sat down on s step and undid her shoe-laces, pulling her shoes off. Her socks followed, and then she dipped her toes into the cool fountain, allowing the water to steam over her tired feet. "The bubbles tickle -It's heavenly."

"I apologize for my girlfriend's bad behavior," Paul said, addressing the statue of Elisha Blackermore. He patted the statue respectfully on the shoulder and then froze. "I'm getting a faint vibe!"

"What?" Benji was puzzled.

"The statues - they are the Blackermores," Paul exclaimed.

"Now how could that be?" Zarah exclaimed. "The statues are out in the bright sunlight. Everyone knows that the Blackermores avoided sunlight."

"The statue of Rachel is wearing a hood," Paul observed. "And Elisha is wearing a deep brimmed hat," Benji added.

"It's not enough," Paul observed. "Unless there was a freak moment of heavy cloud when we killed the Mater Vampire."

"Well we wouldn't know," Zarah said. "We were underground at the time."

"About what time was this?" Benji asked. "Remember I was at the school."

"I dunno," Paul said. "Three-thirty to four perhaps."

"It did come up dull around four o'clock," Benji observed. "The coach moved football training into the gym and we did weights instead of jogging. Of course, most of the bigger boys, like Jaylen and Jamie were off on the hunt."

"Dull, not dark?" Zarah deduced.

Benji nodded.

"Still not dark enough for vampires to be out, and the Blackermores were said to have scorned daylight rings," Paul said.

"They expected the world to conform to their nocturnal habits, not the other way around."

"Look at the tree cover," Zarah said. "There is an avenue all the way from the front door to the fountain. It is around three now, and the shadows are very deep. By four o'clock in the shade of Mount Mystic..."

"It might have been almost dark enough for them in the garden!" Paul exclaimed.

Zarah shivered. "Let's go before it becomes that dull around here today. I don't believe I could bear it." She removed her toes from the fountain and shook her feet dry before replacing her shoes and socks.

The teenagers retrieved their bicycles and pedaled back towards the township of Mystic Evermore. When they got home, it was time for Paul to return to his house for tea. Zarah followed him to the gate for a moment's private farewell.

"What will happen now?" she whispered.

"I don't know," Paul said. "We will have to find an adult - perhaps my father or your gran - who can make the Sheriff believe that the Blackermores are gone. Then she will have to identify their next of kin, if any exist today."

"Gran always said that the Blackermores were vaguely related to the Nevermores," Zarah said. "So perhaps Uncle Nevermore?" She gave Paul a peck on the cheek and sent him on his way.

The conclusion of the Strahan family dinner was the perfect time for Zarah to approach her grandmother for assistance.

"Gran," she said, "Paul and I need your help!"

"You two better behave yourselves for a couple more years," Grandma Strahan returned immediately. "You are far too young to be getting into trouble."

Zarah laughed. "It's not a sex problem," she said.

"I'm glad to hear it," Grandma Strahan said. "After Christy, no one can be too careful around here!"

"Oh I agree," Zarah said. "And Paul already knows I'm not quite ready. He said he would wait a year."

"The right guy will wait many a year for you," Grandma observed.

"Not till we are old and shriveled and dry," Zarah said. "We want to have fun while we are young - admit it - you did!"

"I admit it," Grandmother said. "So what else can I do for you Zarah?"

"We need you and John Booth to talk to Sheriff Favor for us," Zarah said. "Paul and I visited the Blackermore Estate and Paul thinks that Elisha and Rachel Blackermore have become statues."

"About time too," Grandmother Strahan muttered. "They are much older than me, but look so unnaturally young and pretty."

"Funny Grandma," Zarah said.

Grandma Strahan sighed. "Sheriff Favor is somewhat enlightened," She said. "After finding her daughter had become a vampire and that she had dated a vampire herself, Sarah Favor had to accept the existence of vampires around Mystic Evermore. However, I can't go telling her that a boy who thinks he has a strain of witchery in him, believes the Blackermores have suddenly become statues."

"Why ever not?" Zarah asked.

"Because the Sheriff doesn't really believe in witches or some of the other funny things around here," Grandma Strahan said.

"So just report the Blackermore's missing and let the process of the law begin," Zarah begged.

"I guess I can do that," Grandma Strahan said. She picked up the telephone.

Later that evening, Paul and John went down to the police station together with Grandma Strahan and Zarah, for an interview with the Sheriff. Sheriff Favor had already had a big week and wanted nothing more than a lazy night, so she was very cooperative. The official report filed declared that the children had been in the vicinity of the Blackermore Estate, and noticed that all the doors were open and everything seemed deserted.

A visit the following day by the Sheriff and her deputies confirmed the teenager's story; and interviews with the Blackermore's contractors revealed that none of them had received their pay that week or had any other communication from their employers.

An official missing person's file was opened; and the next of kin was granted power of attorney over their estate in the meanwhile. As Paul had suspected, Uncle Nevermore was the certified surviving relative of the Blackermores. The connection was distant and convoluted, but in the absence of any direct offspring of either Elisha or Rachel; all land titles were transferred into the Sebastian's name.

The community were amazed to discover that this property included the entire bulk of Mount Mystic, which had been used as a public park for generations. Apparently it was merely leased from the Blackermores for a very affordable sum by the local government. Uncle Nevermore expressed himself perfectly willing to continue his arrangement with the government and Mount Mystic was able to remain a public park.

The Blackermore Estate was declared a national heritage treasure and opened to the public for educational and recreational purposes. The monies required to manage the estate however, were placed under the administration of Damien Nevermore.

Zarah was puzzled by the charade which required the lands to be held by Uncle Nevermore, when they more rightfully belonged to Damien and Eduard. When she privately expressed her surprise to Paul and Grandma Strahan, they both looked serious.

"I believe it is a precaution," Paul Booth said. "If the land is owned by a human being, vampires and other monsters cannot enter without an invitation."

"Oh," Zarah said.

"There are rumors of caverns beneath Mount Mystic that stretch for miles," Grandmother Strahan said. "It wouldn't do for them to fill with rogue vampires while the Blackermores are trapped inside their statues would it?"

"I guess not," Zarah said. "But what about Damien and Eduard?"

"Damien and Eduard will do their best, but they are younger vampires than the two Blackermores, who were practically royalty so far as vampires go," Paul explained. "The Nevermores need to garner much more power before rogue vampires agree to obey their orders."

"So we have freed our land from the evil Mater Vampire, Henrietta Ermore, but opened it up to possible invasion by vampire gangs?" Zarah exclaimed.

"That's how the Booth witches would understand it," Paul said.

"Two steps forward, one step backwards?" Zarah inquired.

"Yeah, you could say that the Blackermores were necessary evils around here," Grandmother Strahan said. "That's why all the locals turned a blind eye to what they were and all of their peculiarities."

"But this way, with the land in the name of Sebastian

Nevermore, it is protected so long as he survives, or has a living heir," Paul explained.

"Luckily I have just heard Melissa Nevermore is pregnant," Grandma Strahan said with a cackle, and her customary relish for gossip. "That will secure the Blackermore Estates by providing an heir."

"And babies are cute," Zarah was also pleased.

"I have to go now," Paul said. "Errands to run for John and everything. Walk me to the gate?"

He looked at Zarah hopefully.

"Yeah sure," Zarah was quick to stand up and accompany Paul the few steps down the drive-way, where they stood in the shade of a convenient tree to exchange their farewells.

"Carlice told me that she and Jaylen drove Christy interstate to the residence of Eduard's friend where she can live in safety while she learns how to control all her vampire urges," Zarah whispered.

"I am glad," Paul said. "I hope it works out for her." He eyed Zarah quizzically. "You aren't really going to make me wait until next year for another kiss are you?"

Zarah blushed. "Perhaps a little one," she said. "Just before you leave!"

****

PARABLE FIVE: THE ALIEN AMONG US

Ivy Pinkerton had been incredibly depressed ever since her best friend Christy Strahan had fallen into the river and broken her neck. At first the youth all thought Christy was dead, but we heard later Christy had been saved by some miracle, and was in some hospital undergoing rehabilitation. Christy's family were very mysterious about her condition and we knew better than to fool ourselves things would ever be the same again. An injury like Christy suffered would require years of rehabilitation, and as far as most of the senior class knew, Christy would likely never walk again.

(Bridget Etheridge's Journal)

Ivy Pinkerton lived in a little house on the north-eastern fringe of Mystic Evermore with her father Sunny Pinkerton, stepmother Estella, baby brother Liam, and church-going grandmother, old Mrs. Pinkerton.

Ivy's father, Sunny Pinkerton was a market gardener. He was a simple man whose good nature reflected his name. He had been broken hearted when his first wife died while Ivy was a little girl and it had been many years before he had found a new companion.

Estella Pinkerton was slight and bright, and everyone wondered where Sunny Pinkerton had found her. He had literally brought her home from the woods one day and introduced her to the family as his new wife. She had no family living near Mystic Evermore and there was talk she might be one of the faery folk, but that was merely idle gossip. Even if the faery existed, Sunny's conservative mother, who prided herself on setting the moral standards for Mystic Evermore folk, would never have accepted one into their household.

Old Mrs. Pinkerton was one of the town pillars, along with Grandmother Strahan. She was strict and crusty on the outside, but full of love and goodwill on the inside. Her life revolved around her church group and the many social events for which they catered. The most recent events this year had been the sad funeral of Mrs. Etheridge, the bright young wife of Captain Etheridge, and the fantastically romantic wedding of Sebastian Nevermore and his beautiful fiancé Melissa Davis.

Ivy was sitting home that Saturday morning mulling over the evidence that Eduard Nevermore and Lena Lenore had gotten back together during the previous week. As it was only a short time since Eduard's ex-girlfriend Christy had encountered her accident; and that accident had been incurred because she had run from Eduard in alarm and distress over his attentions towards Lena Lenore, Ivy felt this was an insult to her best friend's memory.

Most people however, appeared to be glad that Eduard Nevermore and Lena Lenore, one of the popular power couples at Mystic Evermore high, had re-united. There was a general consensus that Christy was somehow the villain, for going out with Eduard while he and Lena were on a break. Even Zarah Strahan, Christy's little sister whom Ivy had taken to talking to as a reminder of Christy, did not seem very concerned.

Her stepmother Estella hovered into the room with an impossible air of golden cheer, and presented Ivy with a cup of tea and a home baked cookie. Estella's cookies were always rich and crunchy, just the way Ivy's father Sunny liked them. It was like Estella lived to please.

"What's wrong dear?" Estella asked.

Ivy accepted the cookie. "I was thinking about Christy," she said.

"You seem to do that a lot dear," Estella said. "I think perhaps you need to do something for yourself."

Ivy knew exactly what Estella meant. Christy Strahan had been bright and beautiful. Christy had made the friends and then Ivy had also befriended them, Christy had also attracted the boys and Ivy had been content to rest in her shadow. Christy and Ivy had also been friends since kindergarten and Ivy was somewhat lost without her.

"What should I do?" she asked, trying not to think it odd she was taking advice from someone who was young and beautiful, and yet married to Ivy's father. Dad was a nice guy, if not a real prize. When girls in their twenties got over their ultra-romantic stage, they might start going for nice guys, instead of storybook heroes, she mused.

"You could help your gran organise the baby shower for Melissa Nevermore," Estella suggested. "That should be fun, and it's not just for old folks. I said I would help, but you know how some of those church ladies look at me funny."

Ivy laughed despite herself. "Those old biddies look at anyone not born and bred in Mystic Evermore for three generations funny," she agreed. "And I didn't know Melissa was pregnant!"

"Melissa let slip that she and Sebastian were expecting at the last women's meeting," Estella said. "I wasn't there, but your gran told me."

Melissa's husband, Sebastian Nevermore, was commonly known as 'uncle' despite being a young man, because he had adopted his two orphaned nephews, Eduard and Damien Nevermore. No one was quite sure of Damien's age, as he had left school and not yet decided where to go to college. Damien was also responsible for the management of the Blackermore Estate since the disappearance of his distant relatives. Eduard was in his senior year of high school along with Ivy.

"Helping organise the baby shower isn't a bad idea," Ivy mused. "And some of those church biddies are nice enough."

"So off you go then," Estella said. "Liam and I will be alright here, despite your dad being at the Farmer's Market all weekend."

"You must get lonely with Father always working or trading," Ivy said with a sudden flash of compassion for her young stepmother.

Estella shrugged: "I knew Sunny was a hard-working man when I married him!"

Ivy decided to walk down to the Mystic Evermore Episcopalian Church. If she had volunteered to help earlier, Grandma Pinkerton would have given her a lift. However, now Estella would have to bundle Liam into the car seat, except he was currently having a nap, and it was easier for Ivy to just walk. It was also a nice day, and the birds were singing.

When she reached the church, Ivy walked around the back to the hall, where she knew the ladies would be gathered. Gran was happy to see her and put her to work at once, weaving streamers out of strips of crepe paper. The decorations produced by the church ladies were always awesome, as was the party food.

"You know Netta Davis," Gran Pinkerton said, indicating a young girl already plaiting multi-coloured streamers, and Ivy nodded. Netta and Mike Davis were cousins of Melissa Nevermore. Mike was in Ivy's class, and he had been going out with Lena Lenore before the return of Eduard Nevermore to Mystic Evermore. Rumour had it Mike also had his eye on Carlice Favour when she and Jaylen broke up, but she had chosen Fenton Etheridge. Hence Mike was currently girlfriendless and somewhat bitter. Netta was Mike's younger sister and shared her classes with Zarah Strahan.

"How are you today?" Ivy said.

"I'm good," Netta returned brightly. "How are you Ivy?"

Netta was good company. Her mother had been single for some time, because her father ran away to court some socialite up California way. In recent times Mella Davis had begun to date Ben Vaughn, one of the local firefighters, and uncle to Anna Vaughn, one of the senior class. Netta always had stories about all the latest emergencies - and not so emergencies - like when someone called the fire brigade because they got stuck on the toilet - quite literally!

"I'm a bit down," Ivy admitted. "Still missing Christy."

"Yeah, that was shocking," Netta said. "Tell you what, let's play a game and cheer you up."

"What sort of game?" Ivy asked.

"Let's rate the senior boys," Netta said. Being the younger sister of one of the senior guys, Netta was familiar with the senior boys and regarded them somewhat irreverently.

"Okay," Ivy said.

"Who is the hottest?" Netta asked.

"Oh easy," Ivy laughed. "That would be Jaylen Woodgate. He is captain of the football team. Fit, strong and reasonably well off."

"Isn't he hung up on Bridget Etheridge at the moment?" Netta inquired.

"Yeah a bit," Ivy returned. "But I don't think she is interested in return. Who would you nominate?"

"Eduard Nevermore," Netta said. A dreamy look appeared in her eyes. "Although he is already taken by Lena Lenore."

"You would fancy Eduard even after what he did to Christy?" Ivy's voice was sharp.

"Mike told me Christy is going to be okay," Netta said. "Please Ivy, do try to move on."

"I'll tell you a secret," Ivy said. "I haven't heard from Christy since she went to rehab."

"That is a bit strange. Have you asked Zarah?" Netta inquired.

"Yeah, Zarah said Christy would write when she was feeling better," Ivy said.

"Well there you are!" Netta observed.

"But we were BEST friends," Ivy cried. "She should be talking to me."

"Christy must have a lot to deal with, including surgery and physiotherapy every day when she is ready for it," Netta said. "I would give her time if I was her best friend."

"I guess you are right," Ivy said. "Talking of the senior boys - what do you think of Javier Tilton?"

"I'm friends with his little sister Jeroma," Netta said. "But Javier - I've heard he is a bit of a sleaze."

"He did dance with almost every girl at the Apple Festival," Ivy admitted. "But I reckon he's just a new guy being friendly. If there are any other rumours - that is just Eduard Nevermore being mean."

"Who do you think Javier will target now that Lena Lenore is taken?" Netta asked. "Bridget Etheridge? Javier does seem to like them tragic and Bridget just lost her mum."

"Too soon for Bridget," Ivy said. "And Javier wouldn't look at her while Jaylen is interested. They are great friends."

"Fenton Etheridge is too pale," Netta said. "And I reckon he will be back with Carlice Favor soon."

"Probably," Ivy agreed. "They are still good friends."

"That leaves my brother," Netta said. "Mike."

"As if I would tell you what I thought of Mike!" Ivy exclaimed. "That's a trick question."

"You liked him once," Netta suggested mildly.

"We played together when we were kids, not even in high school. As soon as the other girls got curves, Mike was off after them," Ivy admitted.

"I hope you're not sore about that," Netta said.

"Nah, of course not," Ivy said. "I'm used to not being as sexy as the other girls you know."

"I think you play yourself down," Netta said. "Maybe because you always saw yourself as Christy's side-kick."

"Funny, you are the second person to say something like that to me today," Ivy said. She rose from her seat. "I've made a pile of streamers. I'm going to see if Gran needs anything else done."

Ivy crossed the church hall and approached Old Mrs. Pinkerton. "Is there anything else I can do Gran?" she asked.

"Well dear," Old Mrs. Pinkerton said. "You could help me sort the cutlery. I know that doesn't sound like much fun..."

"It's fine," Ivy said. Actually she quite enjoyed sorting things and noting the different patterns on the cutlery sets.

Ivy helped her grandmother sort cutlery, and then volunteered to take the rubbish out to the bins. After that, the ladies were packing up, and Old Mrs. Pinkerton said she would give Ivy a lift home if she were willing to wait for a few minutes. Ivy had experience waiting for her gran when she was with her cronies. Packing up turned into gossiping, which turned into a cuppa together. It was a long process.

"I would like to walk," Ivy said. "The exercise is good for me."

"Alright dear," Old Mrs. Pinkerton said. "I'll see you at home. And remember, you would be welcome at the baby shower if you wanted."

"Thank you," Ivy said.

"I know it's not you young ones' idea of a big Saturday night," Old Mrs. Pinkerton said.

Ivy shook her head. "I don't have a date or anything. There is only the television."

Ivy walked home and as she approached the house she noticed how attractive it was. When her father was not out at the market or on his block of land, he enjoyed do-it-yourself projects around the home. Estella was also a good decorator, and Old Mrs. Pinkerton enjoyed pottering in the garden.

Ivy unlocked the front door and slipped into the house, treading quietly in case Liam was asleep. As she entered the living room, she saw Estella cradling Liam on her lap in one of the big easy chairs. Her stepmother was gazing at the baby with a beatific expression on her face and she appeared to be surrounded by a halo of light. It was a striking cameo, something like an Italian painting of the Virgin Mary.

Estella had not noticed Ivy, and she continued to cradle Liam, murmuring sweet nothings to him. The light surrounding them increased in its intensity, and Ivy glanced around for a lamp or other source of light. There was none.

Ivy cleared her throat: "Estella, I'm home."

Estella looked up and the light surrounding mother and baby faded. Ivy was left wondering whether it had been a reflection from the ornamental mirror on the mantle or a stray beam of sunlight from the window. Perhaps it had been some sort of optical illusion.

"Hello Ivy," Estella said softly. "I was just nursing Liam."

"You looked beautiful," Ivy said. "Like the Madonna and Child." She did not mention the aura-like glow. She may have been mistaken after all.

"Are you going back to the baby shower tonight?" Estella asked.

"I thought I might hang with you and Dad," Ivy said. "Have dinner, watch some television."

"That sounds lovely darling," Estella said. "If Liam will sleep we can have a nice family evening."

As it turned out, the Pinkerton family were lucky. After much bouncing, a good feed, and patting on the back to relieve wind, Ivy's baby brother fell asleep in his cot once tea was finished. Sunny, Estella and Ivy were able to watch almost the full movie in peace before he woke for his night feed.

As Old Mrs. Pinkerton was out, there were able to put on a creepy werewolf movie, *The Howling V*, which was Ivy's all-time favourite. They would not have been able to watch this movie on a night Gran was home because she did not believe in, or approve of such things.

The movie finished just after ten o'clock and Estella was soon occupied with Liam again. Sunny cleared up a little in the kitchen to help his wife in the morning and then retired to bed. Ivy decided to go to bed as well, even though it was relatively early for a Saturday night. In a household with a baby, everyone needed as much sleep as they could possibly get. The last sound she heard as she fell asleep were Liam's gentle gurgles.

Ivy could not say what woke her later that night, or more specifically, in the early hours of the morning. Perchance she had just had enough sleep, or possibly it was the bright moonlight shining through the window. Anyway, she awoke and got up for a drink of water. As she was passing the French doors, walking back towards her bedroom, she glanced out into the night, across the back garden where Sunny's home veggie patch abutted the adjacent woodlands.

After an evening of werewolf movies, Ivy ought to have been frightened by what she saw in the bright moon-light, but she was not.

It was one of the largest dogs she had ever seen, with the beautiful markings of a timber wolf. The canine was loping along the fence line, but as Ivy leaned against the open window, it appeared to stop and sniff her scent wafting through the mesh security screen.

"Who has a beautiful dog like you?" Ivy whispered. She had heard Javier Tilton owned the biggest dog in the county, but she had never seen it. Javier's dog was rarely in evidence.

The wolf sat down on its haunches and opened its mouth to pant. The gesture was so like a grin that Ivy smiled back.

On a sudden impulse, Ivy crossed to the refrigerator and pulled out a lamb chop. Dad always bought plenty of meat and one small offcut surely wouldn't be missed. She opened the back door and threw the piece of meat across the yard. Ivy had played on the school baseball team and wasn't too bad a pitcher. The meat landed right in front of the wolf, who picked it up in his jaws and gulped it down in one bite.

"I'll buy some dog biscuits if you will come back another night," Ivy whispered.

The wolf lifted its muzzle to the moon and howled. Now it sounded wild, and Ivy doubted it really was Javier's pet. No one could own or tame a beauty like that - and yet - one could always try to win its love with food and kindness.

"The moon is not even full yet," Ivy murmured. She had checked the calendar earlier that evening when joking about werewolves with her father, Sunny. It would be a couple of days before the moon waxed, and maybe two more before it waned. "Go in peace wolf-brother!"

The wolf ran off into the woodlands, and presumably across the adjacent farms to one of the larger estates where it could hide. Ivy felt sleepy and cold. Autumn was progressing and the nights were becoming cooler. She decided to return to her warm, soft bed once again.

The next day was Sunday, and the Pinkerton family all attended church. Ivy enjoyed dressing up in her Sunday best, although the neat tailored suit could be classed as quite conservative. Viewing herself in the mirror at the last minute, Ivy decided to remove the preppy looking bow tie from her collar and unbutton one or two buttons to show a little skin.

Grandma Pinkerton looked Ivy up and down when she emerged from her bedroom. "I must say I don't approve of low necks," she said. "But that does show how much you have grown into a young lady."

"I'm sorry Gran," Ivy replied. "The bow-tie was too tight."

"I might be able to find something more suitable for you," Old Mrs. Pinkerton announced and disappeared back into her little unit, which was attached to the rear of the main Pinkerton house.

Ivy sighed. Whatever Gran found for her, she would have to wear, at least once. However, she was surprised and pleased when her grandmother returned with a vintage rhinestone broach.

"I was young once myself," Old Mrs. Pinkerton said. "Now, I will show you something clever."

Ivy had unbuttoned three buttons of her shirt, which led it to gape slightly clumsily. However, she had found that if she only unbuttoned two buttons, she showed no cleavage, and she had wanted to reveal just a hint of curve. Grandmother Pinkerton positioned the broach perfectly between buttons two and three, preventing the gaping effect and yet still revealing the small shadow between the top of Ivy's developing bosoms.

"With a broach like this, you can have any neckline you want," Grandmother Pinkerton said. "You can keep that, I have had it since I was a girl."

"Thanks Gran," Ivy said thrilled. The broach was beautiful, practical and an heirloom. She kissed her grandmother effusively, greatly embarrassing the old lady, who pretended to be in a hurry to get to the car. Family affection had been nearly as forbidden as romantic affection, according to the Puritan heritage her grandmother had inherited.

At church, the sermon was dull and boring; however, Ivy enjoyed looking around at the rest of the congregation. Perhaps in recognition of Melissa Nevermore's pregnancy, the entire Nevermore family was in attendance. Sebastian was looking proud and holding Melissa by the hand. It had been rumoured that both Eduard and Damien had been ill the previous week, but only Eduard showed any signs of lingering weakness. Damien was looking nearly as vibrant as usual.

Netta Davis was there with her mother Mella and brother Mike. Ivy blushed to think how Netta had teased her about Mike the previous day. Her interest in Mike had faded long ago, when she saw how easily distracted he was by the other girls at school.

Noah Bumble was there with Mrs. Woodgate, whom he had been dating for some time now. There was a huge age gap between Noah and Mrs. Woodgate, but they made a cute couple nevertheless. Mrs. Woodgate's son Jaylen was not very regular at church, preferring outdoor activities and exercise, but he was present today, looking bored and somewhat sleepy.

Noah's grandchildren, Javier and Jeroma were sitting with him, but George and Lilibet Tilton were not present. George managed the Mystic Evermore Recreation Centre, and that kept him occupied almost seven days a week. Lilibet Tilton was artistic and not very religious, although she did attend church occasionally.

The Strahan family were absent, as they had not been very sociable since Christy's accident. Grandma Strahan took Sunday mornings off the general store, but did not always attend church. Sheriff Favor was also absent, either on her police duties or catching up on her much needed rest. Her daughter Carlice had no reason to come alone and was likely off doing something with Fenton and Bridget Etheridge.

After church, the youth hung out in the church hall while their parents enjoyed tea and coffee in the hall. This wasn't because they weren't allowed to snack, but because it was more suited to the teenage temperament to be leaning against the wall, pretending to be cool, than sitting inside listening to their elders interminable gossip.

Ivy found herself talking to Javier, Jeroma and Jaylen. Javier, who insisted his name was said with a "J" and not the Hispanic "H", was the new boy in town and had not yet selected a girlfriend from amongst the Mystic Evermore crowd. He was checking them all out and his extravagant attentions were slightly embarrassing whenever he focused on Ivy.

Jaylen was every high school girl's crush, as he was the captain of the football team and their star player. Ivy had never in her wildest dreams considered taking him seriously, but today she found his brown eyes liquid and appealing. There was no denying he had a certain animal magnetism. When he invited Ivy to come and watch his football practice Monday night, she found herself saying that she would think about it.

Ivy half expected Jeroma, who hero-worshiped Jaylen, to be jealous; but Jeroma obviously considered Jaylen family, as their grandfather was dating Mrs. Woodgate, and added her warm invitation to Jaylen's.

"Oh do come along – it's fun even though we only watch," Jeroma cried. "And Jaylen gives us a lift home afterwards. Sometimes we stop for milkshakes!"

"Wouldn't your car be full then?" Ivy asked.

"Jaylen's four-wheel-drive can fit five at a squeeze," Jeroma explained.

"We won't be having a late night this week," Jaylen said. "I have a lot of homework to do. I must keep my grades up or I can't play football."

"And the moon will be full by then," Ivy added dreamily. Jaylen, Jeroma and Javier looked at Ivy in obvious astonishment. Ivy shrugged, trying to cover her confusion. "I don't know why I said that!"

Ivy did know why she had said it actually. It was because of the werewolf movies and the beautiful dog she had seen the night before. However, she could not mention that to her friends. They would laugh at her.

In the afternoon, Ivy walked down to the Strahan General Store to buy dog biscuits. The majority of the shops in Mystic Evermore were closed all day Sunday, but Grandma Strahan insisted on opening between two and four pm, in case anyone needed medications or other essentials. While she was in the store, Ivy lingered a few moments to talk to Grandma Strahan and ask whether the family had heard anything from Christy.

Once again, Ivy received unsatisfying answers such as: "Christy is doing as well as can be expected", "It will take a while," and "We don't know when Christy will be back, she will write or call when she is strong enough."

Ivy understood she ought to be patient, because Christy's injuries had been so shockingly severe, but she resented the fact that the family would not even tell her which hospital Christy had gone to for treatment. She lingered for some time in the city square, window shopping through closed windows and wishing her long-time friend

Christy were with her to make the outing actually fun.

Ivy then turned for home and began to walk towards the northern edge of the suburbs. She had almost reached her home when Jaylen drove past. He slowed the four wheel drive and came to a halt beside her, winding down the window.

"You want to be careful," Jaylen said. "It's getting dark. Anything could be out here."

"Oh it won't be really dark for another hour," Ivy said. "Where are you going at this time of afternoon anyway?"

"To the Woodgate Estate," Jaylen said. "I enjoy camping on the grounds."

"Alone?" Ivy inquired.

"Sometimes I take Javier," Jaylen said. "Although then Jeroma starts wanting to tag along, which can be a problem."

"I see how it would be," Ivy observed dryly.

"Hop in, I'll drive you the rest of the way home," Jaylen offered.

"It's only a few blocks," Ivy objected, but she climbed into the vehicle anyway.

Jaylen smelled warm and somewhat musky in the close confines of the interior. Ivy had to reprimand her mind because it wanted to wander into forbidden territory. She was sure that the captain of the football team could have any girl he wanted and had no need to be looking at her in a romantic light.

"What do you have there?" Jaylen inquired, pointing to her shopping.

"Oh nothing," Ivy said, trying to put the bag down out of sight.

"Dog biscuits?" Jaylen guessed, although Ivy was not sure how he knew. "So if you meet the big bad wolf you are going to feed it and hope it doesn't eat you?"

"I saw a big dog last night," Ivy said, ignoring the pun based on *Little Red Riding Hood*. "It was beautiful - like a great wolf."

"If you see it again," Jaylen said. "Please play it safe. Don't open the door to it."

"I don't think it would hurt me," Ivy objected. "I threw it some meat."

"If it is the one I'm thinking of - it's wild!" Jaylen said. "Not a pet. You don't know what it might do."

"How do you know?" Ivy asked curiously. "Have you seen it while you are out camping?"

"Perhaps," Jaylen was non-committal, and his hands held the steering wheel tightly while his eyes stared straight ahead at the road.

They pulled up at the Pinkerton house.

"Here is your home," Jaylen said. "I'll see you tomorrow Ivy."

"Okay," Ivy said. "Thanks for the lift."

Ivy turned and began to walk up her driveway to the front door.

Jaylen sat and watched her until she reached the lighted steps, and then revved the engine. He took off fast and left a set of skid marks on the roadside.

Ivy took an old plate Estella did not use for serving food anymore and filled it with dog biscuits. She placed the plate on the back veranda and went inside to have her tea. The biscuits were still there when she went to bed that night, but somehow had all gone in the morning. The plate was empty; and Sunny, Estella and Grandma Pinkerton all denied throwing the biscuits away.

****

Monday morning at school, Ivy noticed a subtle change in her classmate's attitudes. She had sat virtually alone at school since Christy's accident, but first period, Javier slid into the seat beside her. Ivy would have thought this was just his girl-hunting ways, but second period Jaylen sat in the desk next to her. Fourth period, her companion was Carlice and fifth period it was Bridget Etheridge. Sixth period, even her old playmate Mike Davis sat down beside her.

Lunch time Ivy was invited to join Fenton Etheridge and Carlice Favor at the table commonly reserved for the 'A list' popular seniors. The only people at that table who did not speak to her were Eduard Nevermore and Lena Lenore, who were too absorbed in each other to notice anyone around them.

After school Ivy decided she may as well visit the football field to watch practice like Jaylen had suggested. When she reached the field, she found the bleachers were already occupied by Jeroma Tilton and Bridget Etheridge. Ivy hesitated, but Jeroma saw her and waved.

"Come and join the official Jaylen Woodgate fan club," Jeroma said.

Ivy was surprised when Bridget slid aside to allow Ivy to sit between her and Jeroma.

"Official fan club?" Ivy inquired.

"As opposed to the unofficial fan club over there," Jeroma said, indicating the cluster of girls from every grade hanging around the edge of the football field gawking at the hot players. "We are the ones who have actually been invited."

"I see," Ivy said.

Bridget appeared a little embarrassed. "Actually I don't consider myself a fan club member," she muttered.

"Jaylen likes you to be here," Jeroma remarked, as if that settled the matter.

Carlice Favor arrived with Lena Lenore. Carlice's boyfriend Fenton played football occasionally, although he was more of a track and field star, and Eduard Nevermore was a strong, regular football player.

"How is everybody?" Carlice asked.

"Good thanks," the other girls chorused.

Ivy had to admit that it was entertaining watching the boys perform their drills. In fact, more happened than in a regular match, because there were structured skills instruction and practice. She actually learned a little about the game while watching.

Towards the end of practice, Ivy was beginning to wonder how they would all fit into Jaylen's car, but Damien Nevermore came and took Bridget away. Lena left with Eduard, who also had a car, and Fenton and Carlice jumped in the back seat. That left only Jeroma and Ivy to travel home with Jaylen.

True to his word, Jaylen drove Ivy straight home. The drive was without incident, except once he had to slam on the brakes when a huge bear shambled out of the woods and across the road. Jaylen muttered it was unusual so close to the built up area, and Jeroma returned that she had heard bears even raided bins in some areas.

"Not around Mystic Evermore they don't," Jaylen muttered under his breath, and Jeroma was too smart to argue with her idol. Jaylen hit the hooter hard, and the bear ambled away, intimidated by the noise.

"Thanks for the lift," Ivy said, jumping out of the car.

"That's alright," Jaylen said. "Thanks for coming to watch. We will do something after practice another time."

"Sure," Ivy agreed easily.

Jaylen drove off with Jeroma. Ivy knew that not only were their families connected, but the two lived within a stone's throw of each other on the same street.

Tuesday morning the phone rang early, and Grandma Pinkerton answered it. She listened for a few minutes and then spoke sharply, sounding quite shocked. "Of course, I'll be there immediately."

Grandma hung up and spoke to Ivy and Estella. "That was Sebastian Nevermore on the phone," she said. "It is bad news. Melissa has been mauled by an animal - possibly a wolf or bear. I have to go up to the hospital, she has lost a lot of blood and I am listed as a compatible donor."

Estella and Ivy looked at each other in alarm. "What about the baby?" Estella cried.

"At this stage, no one knows," Grandma Pinkerton announced. Estella turned to Ivy: "Ivy I hate to ask you to miss school - but could you babysit Liam for me this morning? I would like to go to the hospital and see Melissa. She has always been nice to me."

"I would love to babysit my little brother," Ivy said. "And schoolwork can wait."

"He might be a little bit fussy missing me," Estella said. "But there is a bottle of expressed breast milk in the refrigerator. Be sure to heat it gently using a bowl of hot water."

"I know the way," Ivy said. She did not look after her young brother that often, but was very proud of herself whenever she was trusted with Liam.

"Thank you - thank you so much," Estella said, and rushed off with Grandmother Pinkerton.

Sunny had already gone to work in the gardens, so Ivy was left alone with the baby. She turned the television on for company. At first there were the regular morning cartoons, but then the news bulletin came on.

The incident where a local resident had been mauled by a wild animal was all over the morning bulletin, although Melissa's name had not yet been released. There was some speculation that the animal that attacked her might have been rabid.

Liam slept like an angel in his cot for several hours and then began to cry. Ivy went into the bedroom and picked him up. She balanced him on her hip while she heated the bowl of water, and placed the bottle in it to warm up by convection. This method of warming had been taught to Estella by her grandmother, and ensured that the milk was never hot enough to burn the baby's mouth. Then Ivy sat down in Estella's favorite chair to feed Liam.

Liam sucked greedily at the bottle. Ivy had learned if she allowed him, he would drink the whole bottle with one gulp, but then he would be full of wind. So she deliberately stopped him at one minute intervals and patted his back, waiting for the soft burps. After the bottle was finished, Ivy put Liam down on the floor to play. He rolled onto his tummy and tried to support himself with his arms.

Liam was so little and so cute, Ivy lay down on the floor in front of him. He wasn't yet crawling, but he tried to reach towards her. After about five minutes, Liam became tired and frustrated. Ivy picked him up and judged it was time to check the nappy. A stinky one told her everything was in working order.

After the nappy change, Ivy wrapped Liam up in his cuddle rug again. She knew he would take some amusing until Estella returned, so she shook a rattle in front of his eyes. He reached out a little hand and tried to clutch, but his grip was not strong enough. Ivy laid the rattle on his stomach and he patted at it. The rattle clattered and Liam laughed.

Then the strangest thing happened. Liam laughed again and began to glow. At first, Ivy thought the sun was coming through the curtain and warming the two of them, but then she noticed it was Liam himself who was glowing. She checked his clothes for little LEDs, like the ones on his battery operated flashing shoes. There were none that Ivy could detect. She felt his forehead, he was warm, but not too hot.

Ivy had never seen a baby glow before and the phenomena didn't seem to be described in any of the baby books Estella had collected while she was pregnant. Ivy was a little frightened, so she put Liam down in his cot. He snuffled a few protests and then fell asleep again. The glow faded as he lost consciousness.

Ivy returned to the lounge room, where the television was now playing a mid-day movie. She sat down and tried to lose herself in the story. A few minutes later, Estella returned and Ivy greeted her with relief.

"Your grandmother stayed at the hospital in case they needed blood again," Estella said. "Although she really ought not to donate twice in a row."

"Estella," Ivy said urgently. "I really need to talk to you about something."

"Yes?" Estella was surprised.

"When I was playing with Liam earlier - he glowed!" Ivy began to feel silly even saying it. Maybe she had been hallucinating, but Estella looked matter-of-fact.

"I've been trying to teach him not to do that," Estella said.

"You knew?" Ivy exclaimed.

"He does it when he is happy," Estella said. "He hasn't learned to mask his feelings like the rest of us yet."

"I don't think I could glow if I tried," Ivy said. "People don't glow."

"As he is your little brother, and he would need you if anything happened to me," Estella said, "I have to tell you some things. After school when Grandma is home to babysit Liam."

"I can't go to school now," Ivy exclaimed. "There are only two hours left."

"Those are two classes and the chance to collect all your notes from the other classes," Estella remarked practically.

Ivy's stepmother had never been particularly strict before, but that afternoon she put her foot down and insisted on putting Liam in the car seat and driving Ivy to the tail end of the school day. Estella was also ready and waiting when Ivy was dismissed from school. Ivy crossed to the car and climbed in, noting that Liam was not in the car.

"Grandma must be home!" Ivy observed.

"Yes," Estella said. "Your grandmother is watching Liam, which makes this the ideal time for us to have a talk."

"What if he glows for her?" Ivy was concerned.

"I doubt Liam will glow for your gran - she doesn't seem the glowing type," Estella observed practically.

Ivy laughed. "Where are we going?"

"I have something to show you," Estella said.

Ivy expected they would go to one of the more exclusive coffee shops in town where they could get a private booth for a mother-daughter talk like other families. However, Estella kept on driving.

She drove past the Pinkerton house, past the Farmer's Market and past the Old Mill Farm. Finally she stopped at a point where the woodlands bordered the Woodgate Estate.

"Is it wise to go in there at this hour?" Ivy asked. The shadows were lengthening and the woods were beginning to look remarkably dark.

"We will be alright," Estella said. She climbed out of the car and Ivy followed.

Estella locked the car and led the way into the woods. Ivy noticed that her stepmother walked with confidence and appeared to know exactly where she was going. Ivy was surprised. Estella had never seemed the 'stroll in the woods type', but then she never really seemed any type, except Ivy's father's ideal bride.

On a point where Ivy estimated the adjacent Woodgate Estate met the prime farming land, Estella paused and walked towards a seemingly faceless rock. She raised her hand and a hatch slid aside in the rock wall, allowing Estella to step inside.

Ivy hurriedly stepped inside the rock as well. She suddenly found herself looking at the outside world through a huge set of curved windows. Some sort of console was in the center of the space, and cocoon-like beds lined the lower halves of the wall. At one point, there appeared to be a high-tech food preparation area, and another point offered ablution facilities.

"What is this?" Ivy exclaimed.

"It is my home," Estella said.

Ivy glanced around in amazement. "Exactly how old are you Estella?"

Estella shrugged. "I don't know," she said. "I woke up here last year."

"Really?" Ivy was looking for the trick.

"Yes really," Estella insisted. "Your father was knocking on my front door. He was the most beautiful man I had ever seen."

"Don't you mean the only man you had ever seen?" Ivy observed cynically.

"No, I think there is a paternal-figure somewhere in my memory," Estella said. "And Sunny really is deserving. I don't think I would have woken for anyone else."

"Like *Sleeping Beauty*?" Ivy exclaimed.

Estella smiled sweetly. "I like that story, I read it to Liam."

"Seriously Estella - What are you? An alien or a science experiment?" Ivy inquired.

"An alien I think," Estella admitted." I can make the ship hover a little using my powers."

"Powers?" Ivy asked.

"Small things - like channeling electricity," Estella admitted. "I can also heal a little using the body's natural electricity."

"No way!" Ivy cried.

"Yes way," Estella asserted. "Have you had a cough or cold since I married your father?"

"I don't think so," Ivy had to admit. "Why didn't you heal Melissa Nevermore then?"

"Her injuries were too severe, she needed the hospital," Estella explained. "I may be able to help reduce the scarring later."

"Oh my, I can't believe this!" Ivy had to sit down, and plonked herself at one of the consoles. A confusing row of buttons stared back at her.

"I am human enough to breed with your father however," Estella said. "We - err had Liam the normal way."

"The normal way," Ivy muttered. She blushed at the idea of her dad having sex, even though she knew it must have happened as he was newly married. "I remember, you went to hospital like any other mother."

"I like to think I am like any other mother," Estella asserted. "But Liam is - half whatever I am."

"I see," Ivy agreed.

"I don't know how different to a normal boy he will be growing up, and I will need your help as his big sister if you can accept all this," Estella begged.

"It's a shock," Ivy said. "They say weird things happen around Mystic Evermore - but they usually mean wild animal attacks and bizarre crimes. Not resident aliens."

"Please try to think of me as your father's wife again," Estella cried.

"I will when I can," Ivy ventured. "And Liam will always be my little brother."

"Good!" Estella said. "That's all I can ask. If you would be my friend as well, I would be thrilled, but I don't know if I can expect..."

"What's that?" Ivy cried, pointing to a lumbering creature outside the spaceship's viewing window.

"I don't know," Estella said. "But it can't get in here."

"Are you sure?" Ivy clutched at her stepmother in fright. "It's sniffing around."

"I'm sure the ship is secure," Estella promised. "The creature is ugly isn't it? It must be the thing that attacked Melissa Nevermore."

"It's trying to get inside," Ivy cried as the spaceship rocked from the impact of a heavy body.

"It must be able to smell us somehow," Estella whispered. "Be very still and very quiet."

The girls clung together in the cabin of the small spaceship, trying to be still and trying to outwait the monster. However, the ugly creature sat down outside and began picking at its paws. They had great claws, and there was dried dirt around the pads. The sight was gross.

"Does your ship have any weapons?" Ivy whispered.

"I never found any," Estella returned. "I think I'm from a peaceful planet."

"Surely it would have something - just for protection," Ivy speculated.

"Does Sunny's car?" Estella asked. "It's just a vehicle - for transport."

Ivy shook her head in defeat: "But we cannot spend the whole night here."

"I spent many a night here while Sunny and I were courting," Estella admitted. "But I have not expressed enough milk for Liam."

"Gran will find some formulae for him," Ivy suggested.

"I don't know whether formulae is good for him," Estella objected. "Unfortunately there is little I can do. I will text Sunny - he must not come looking for me with that out there."

"Dad is very brave," Ivy said.

"Still we don't want to see him mauled before our eyes by that zombie were-bear or whatever it is," Estella replied practically.

Estella activated her mobile phone and typed a suitably vague message about visiting the hospital, and staying up there possibly until morning. If Ivy's father went looking for them at all, the message would at least send him to a lighted, safe institution where a couple of visitors could easily miss each other among the corridors.

As Estella closed her phone, it let out a slight beep and the creature outside appeared to hear. It stirred and the girls clung together even tighter in their fear. Ivy could even hear herself breathing and the thump of her own heart-beat. Estella's bodily functions seemed more subtle, and Ivy could not hear anything. Ivy and Estella clung together in the dark, until they fell asleep underneath the center console.

It was something like midnight when Ivy woke and raised her head. Luckily she sensed the presence of the console before hitting her head sharply against it, and escaped with a little bump. She shook Estella to wake her.

"Look!" Estella followed Ivy's pointing finger.

"It's the dog," Ivy murmured.

Shining silver in the moon-light, outlined in the viewing window were two alert looking wolf ears and a sharp muzzle surrounded by a shaggy coat of hair.

"I've seen it out here before," Estella admitted. "But only when the moon is close to full."

"I don't think it would hurt us," Ivy whispered. "And I'm sure it would chase the bear away."

"I think I can find the car in the dark," Estella whispered. "If you are willing to try."

They crept to the hatch, which slid open at Estella's touch and Ivy whistled softly for the dog. The wolf ran up to Ivy and snuffled at her hand.

"I'm sorry I don't have any biscuits," Ivy whispered, but remembering her afternoon recess, she pulled out the second half of her sandwich. "Here."

Estella clucked in soft disapproval that Ivy had been too dainty to eat her whole sandwich, but she had to admit the leftovers were convenient in the current circumstances.

"Please stay with us," Ivy whispered, scratching the dog behind the ears.

The wolf cocked its head and the girls stepped out of the spaceship into the dark woods. Ivy's heart beat with fear, but she sensed that the bear-like creature wouldn't approach while the dog was close. Estella set off walking at a fast pace towards where they had left the car. She strode through the woods with confidence, and

Ivy wondered whether her stepmother had other powers she had not yet mentioned, like infra-red or night vision.

It only took a quarter of an hour to reach the car, but it seemed like an eternity. The wolf padded alongside Ivy, and she rested one hand on its back. Ivy knew that it was larger than a normal pet dog, but she was surprised how little she had to stoop to reach the dog's furry back. In fact, at one point, she almost felt as if she was reaching upwards to touch its shaggy coat. It was almost as though the wolf had become gigantic in order to protect them.

Estella and Ivy reached the side of the road where they had parked the car, and there was a frightening moment when Estella fumbled with the keys. Finally, the car was unlocked and they were both inside with the doors shut securely around them and the windows wound up tight. Estella turned on the ignition and then hit the light switch.

The wolf was lit up by the car headlights. It was grey and white with small flacks of rust in its coat. Its eyes glinted green and wild as it turned and loped away back into the woods. One moment it had been their faithful companion and guardian, and the next it was gone.

"I'm so glad the wolf came for us," Ivy whispered.

Estella was concentrating grimly on warming the engine and turning onto the road. A dark shadow that the girls knew was not the wolf lumbered out of the bushes, and Estella pressed the accelerator pedal down, increasing their speed until they had left the fearful hulk far behind. A few minutes later, they turned onto the main road into Mystic Evermore and then drove into their own driveway.

Ivy and Estella were both glad to see that Sunny had left the lights on for them. The yellow glow of the porchlight spread across the verandah and gave them the courage to get out of the car and make the short sprint to the house. Then Sunny was opening the door and hugging his wife and daughter.

"I'm so glad you are back," Sunny said. "I left the fields well before dark, there is talk that all residents should be careful until the creature that attacked Melissa is destroyed."

"We are glad to be back," Ivy said. Neither Ivy nor Estella mentioned their visit to the woods. Ivy figured Sunny knew Estella's secret because he had courted her while she was living in the space ship, however, she expected her stepmother would explain to him in her own time.

"Has Liam been good?" Estella asked.

Sunny nodded. "He went to sleep for his grandmother, but I guess he will be waking for his night feed soon."

****

Wednesday at school Jaylen sat with Ivy second period, and escorted her back to her locker at recess time, where the talk was mostly about Melissa Davis and the bear attack. Then he rested a paw-like hand on Ivy's arm and whispered, "I'm glad that you are okay," before he left her at the lockers.

After that, Jaylen was off, quickly disappearing to strut around with his football buddies. Ivy was left gazing after him and thinking oddly enough about a grey and rust colored wolf that appeared only during the full moon. She shook herself and focused upon sorting her books for the next periods.

Seniors ought to be at school to study, however, at Mystic Evermore High many other things appeared to take priority. On Thursday and Friday, more attention was devoted to what they were doing date-night Friday night, and party-night Saturday night. Once Ivy had not worried very much about the social drama, because she did what Christy did, unless Christy wanted to be alone with Eduard. Now Ivy was alone among all the class social politics.

She was heading towards the senior table at lunch, keen to enter into all the chit-chat and perhaps secure herself an invitation for the weekend, when Netta hailed her.

Ivy did not want to be rude, so she stopped and paused beside the junior's lunch table.

"Please sit down," Netta begged.

"Alright," Ivy settled into one of the seats. "What is it Netta?"

"Mum has suggested that we use the garage as a games room while the Sheriff's safety guidelines are in force," Netta began. Although the Sheriff had not issued a formal curfew, she had announced some guidelines designed to protect community residents from injuries like those sustained by Melissa Nevermore.

"That sounds great," Ivy said.

"So Friday night I am allowed to invite two friends," Netta

continued. "I have chosen you and Jeroma Tilton."

"Who is Mike inviting?" Ivy asked.

"He is inviting Javier Tilton and Wilson Booth," Netta explained.

Ivy was disappointed. She had hoped to somehow wangle and invitation to some activity she would have in common with Jaylen Woodgate. She wasn't sure whether anything other than friendship was actually happening there, but he had invited her to watch the football practice. On the other hand, she could hardly refuse to visit Netta as their families were very close at church.

"I would love to come," Ivy said. "Are you sure Mike wouldn't consider inviting Jaylen?"

"Someone seems to have a crush," Netta joked, right in front of the other juniors! Ivy flushed bright red. "Unfortunately Jaylen has something on Friday night with his mother."

"Oh okay," Ivy said, reflecting that Netta could be quite a brat at times. "I'll see you Friday night then."

"Remember, don't walk over," Netta said. "Get your dad to drive you - and pick you up afterwards."

"Yes ma'am," Ivy said and rose to her feet. She walked quickly towards the seniors table, where she slid into a seat between Carlice and Jaylen. "How are you guys?"

"Would you believe," Carlice complained, "That there is a meeting of the Agrarian Council Friday night and Mrs. Lockwood has decided that us kids should attend, at least the dinner part?"

"Not really," Ivy mused. Even though her family were not pedigreed enough to be involved in the Agrarian Council, Ivy knew it was rare for the adult members to involve their children.

"Apparently Damien Nevermore is being inducted onto the council and that is a big deal," Jaylen explained.

"Damien Nevermore eh?" Ivy murmured. Although the Nevermore's were among Mystic Evermores' oldest surviving families, they had not been involved in the Agrarian Council for some years.

"Bridget will be Damien's date of course," Carlice added. "And Fenton will be mine."

"Are Bridget and Damien back together?" Ivy asked curiously.

"No," Jaylen said. "They are good friends, since Bridget decided he was too old for her."

"Damien is just university age," Ivy objected.

Carlice shook her head. "There is more to Damien Nevermore than meets the eye."

"Yeah," Ivy said. "There seems to be a lot of that going around." (Stepmothers and little brothers who are aliens, monster bears and guardian angel dogs, to say the very least.) "Are you and Fenton back together?" she asked Carlice.

"I'm hoping," Carlice said. "Ah there he is now."

Fenton put his lunch down on the table and sat in the chair on the other side of Carlice.

"What took you so long?" she asked.

"Just talking to Eduard," Fenton said, indicating Eduard Nevermore who had arrived at the table beside him. "Do you know some people are worried that the attack on Melissa Nevermore might not have been random?"

"How can a bear attack not be random?" Ivy was puzzled.

"It might be possible for someone to train the bear, infect the creature with rabies and set it after Melissa or something," Eduard said. He sounded fierce, and for a moment Ivy thought his mouth looked funny, almost as if he had two fangs hanging out of each side of his lower lip. "If I find anyone has hurt my aunt deliberately..."

"But why would they?" Ivy exclaimed innocently. "Melissa is such a lovely lady - and expecting a baby."

"Well," Fenton said. "Now that local billionaires Elisha and Rachel Blackermore have disappeared, Uncle Nevermore is the titleholder for one of the largest packages of land held in private hands in the state of Georgia."

"Really? Who gave you that statistic?" Ivy inquired.

Fenton shrugged. "It's just what people say."

"I can sorta believe it," Jaylen said. "The Blackermore Estate makes the Woodgate Estate look like a suburban backyard, and they say the land originally included Mount Mystic, which is leased to local government as a park. I'm not sure what else the Blackermores owned..."

"So," Fenton paused significantly, "That could make Melissa and Uncle targets for bad guys. No wonder Eduard is worried."

"We just have to hope Melissa recovers," Ivy said. "Have you heard about the baby yet Eduard?"

"Her body suffered a massive shock, but she didn't go into spontaneous labor," Eduard said. "The doctors are hopeful the pregnancy will continue healthily."

"That is a relief," Ivy exclaimed. She turned to Jaylen. "So who is your date for the Agrarian Council dinner?"

"I don't need a date," Jaylen's eyes were unfathomable. "What are you doing Friday night?"

"I'm going to a games evening in Netta and Mike's garage," Ivy admitted.

"I wish I was," Jaylen said. "It sounds like a lot more fun than the Agrarian Council meeting."

"Maybe Saturday?" Ivy suggested.

"I don't know what I'll be doing Saturday yet," Jaylen said. "Coach mentioned something about a weekend practice to make up for missing evening practices."

"That will involve most of the guys if it happens, wont it?" Ivy said.

"I guess," Jaylen said. "I will let you know."

On impulse, Ivy reached out and brushed a finger along the line created by Jaylen's short cropped hair just above and around his ear. Jaylen looked at Ivy out of the corner of his eye, but did not push her hand away. There was a small smile hovering around the corner of his mouth.

****

When Ivy arrived at the Davis house Friday night, she found that the Davises had a large garage, part of which was permanently occupied by a table tennis table. Another part was a bit of a reading nook defined by a large shaggy rug, and scattered with cushions and bean bags.

Then there was Mella Davis' metal tool cupboard, which would be out of bounds for the games. Mella had parked the car outside to allow the teens to use the remainder of the garage for more active games. The garage was wired to the mains electricity, which was somewhat of a luxury for an outbuilding.

"This is cool," Ivy exclaimed.

"I'm only delivering snacks," Mella Davis, Mike and Netta's mum, announced. "I'm going to be up at the house, I trust you kids to behave yourselves, you are all old enough."

"The sandwiches look wonderful," Ivy said. She had already had tea, but she had no doubt that she would get hungry again; and the selection of biscuits, cakes and snacks made her mouth water in anticipation. "Thank you Ms. Davis."

"She didn't say old enough for what!" Javier Tilton scoffed after Mella had left the garage.

Mike gave him a friendly shove. "None of that, young Javier. We all know you have a one track mind."

"Not at all," Javier declared. "I also play a mean hand at table tennis."

"You are on!" Mike exclaimed, and the two boys began to play a match.

Ivy greeted Wilson Booth. Wilson had been a member of their senior class until he had dropped out earlier this year. He was not very academic, and had also experienced harassment for being African-American. Ivy could not believe some teachers were still racist in the twenty-first century.

"How have you been?" she asked.

"Really good," Wilson replied. "I am enjoying my apprenticeship as a plumber with Robbie Strahan."

"That is great," Ivy exclaimed. She had a soft spot for Wilson Booth, because he used to like Christy Strahan. He had lost her to the more glamorous Eduard Nevermore of course. "Do you ever hear anything about Christy?"

"No," Wilson said. "The Strahan's are really closed mouthed about her whereabouts. I can only conclude it means her recovery will take a long time."

"Mm," Ivy murmured.

"I have a plan though," Wilson said. "If I can somehow find out where Christy is - I will go and visit her."

"You are still interested in Christy?" Ivy was surprised.

"There isn't much that could put me off her," Wilson asserted.

"Well I hope you do find her," Ivy said. "That could be very interesting. Very interesting indeed."

"Over here Ivy," Netta called, and Ivy was obliged to join Netta and Jeroma in a game of scrabble. Meanwhile Wilson joined Javier and Mike in the battle for table tennis supremacy.

After the girls had played board games for several rounds, and the boys had exhausted their interest in table tennis and darts, the teens settled down to drink ginger beer and eat the snacks.

"What shall we do now?" Netta asked.

Javier Tilton pulled several packets of cards out of the pockets of his voluminous coat. It made Ivy, who was slightly high on sugar and soft drink, giggle and wonder what else he kept in there.

"Has anyone played battle cards?" Javier asked.

"Yeah sure," Mike said. "Show me what you have got."

Javier opened the top pack and displayed its contents.

Mike whistled. "I've got a couple of packs here in the box, but nothing as ace as that in them."

"I did a few tournaments back in Chicago and won some special cards," Javier said. "Unfortunately there is not much opportunity around here."

"We will teach the others how to play," Mike said. "We have four packs in total… so first four play, and the two with the lowest scores drop out."

"I will be one of the first four," Ivy volunteered. Javier handed her a pack of cards.

"There you go," Javier said. "That is a very good pack. You should have a fighting chance with that one."

The first round was fought between Mike and Wilson, and Jeroma and Ivy. Predictably, Wilson and Ivy, who had never played battle cards before, had the lowest scores and had to drop out.

The next round saw Mike play Netta, while Javier played Jeroma. The two brother and sister matches were hard fought. While the cards belonged to the boys, they had often played with their sisters, so the girls knew most of the boys' tricks!

Finally, Netta bested Mike and Javier beat Jeroma. That left Javier and Netta to play the final match. Javier won, but everyone agreed Netta had put up a valent fight.

"Let's play truth or dare," Netta suggested, when the card games were finished.

"So long as the dares are all good fun and nothing that could actually hurt anybody," Ivy agreed.

Wilson looked amused. "Alright," he said.

Ivy felt Mike and Javier eying her speculatively, and flushed hot all over. It was rare that any boys looked at her like that, and Mike had not done so before she had changed her way of dressing.

"Truth or dare Ivy," Javier said. "Have you ever been kissed?" His voice was as smooth as velvet and Ivy felt herself momentarily drawn to him. While kissing Javier wasn't something Ivy normally wanted to do, she felt her pulse begin to race and visions of him and her down on the cushions swam into her head.

"Not really," Ivy muttered, looking down at the floor. While Ivy thought something might be starting with Jaylen, she was still basically un-kissed.

"Truth or dare Mike," Wilson said. "Have you ever kissed Carlice Favor?"

"Yes," Mike admitted. "It wasn't quite what I expected either!"

"Truth or dare Wilson," Netta asked.

"Dare!" Wilson said. His eyes were glinting. In his experience, the truth could be a troublesome thing.

"Climb up and show us how long you can hang from the rafter," Netta said. They had said no dangerous dares, but the rafters in the garage were not very high. It was basically a test of muscle endurance, like a chin-up.

Wilson made a standing leap from the floor and caught the rafter. He hung there for several minutes, his muscles bulging.

"Wow!" Netta's eyes were big. "You have great muscles Wilson!"

"Truth or dare Netta," Jeroma said.

"Dare," Netta said.

"Kiss the boy of your choice," Jeroma instructed.

Netta's brother Mike was present to provide a safe option for a kiss on the cheek, but Netta turned her gaze towards Javier. Javier, who had seemed so hot about the idea when asking Ivy whether she had ever been kissed, suddenly became very coy. Maybe it was because Javier was all talk no action; or maybe because he had little interest in junior girls.

Netta, on the other hand, was looking quite keen. She was accustomed to hanging out with her older brother's friends, and they were usually indulgent towards her. Moreover, the girl was hot for her first kiss, and Javier was the new and mysterious boy in town.

"Pucker up," Mike said. "You two have to kiss."

Netta leaned forward and placed her hands on Javier's shoulders. She tilted her head slightly sideways and pressed her rosebud mouth against Javier's lips. Javier sat rigidly still, and did not respond. Netta finished giving him a smooch and drew back humiliated.

"You didn't kiss me back," Netta whispered.

"It's just a game," Javier said. "You didn't expect us to really 'pash' did you?"

"I don't know what I expected," Netta whispered. She scrambled to her feet and crossed the garage to the darts board. "Ivy, Jeroma - would you like to play darts with me?"

"Sure," Ivy said. She also climbed to her feet and crossed the garage floor. "Are you all right Netta?"

"Yeah," Netta said, but there were tears close to the surface. "I thought Javier Tilton was looking for a girlfriend."

"I think he is only looking amongst the seniors," Ivy said. "Besides, Javier wasn't your number one pick when we talked about hot guys last week."

"No, well Eduard is taken by Lena," Netta said.

"Well what about the boys in your class?" Ivy suggested.

Netta shrugged. "They are kids."

"What about Nathan Vaughn?" Ivy asked.

"Too short," Netta said. "He hasn't commenced his growth spurt yet."

"Benji Strahan?" Ivy probed.

"Worse, even younger," Netta said. "And I think he likes Jeroma."

"Someone will come along," Ivy said. "You will see."

Saturday morning Ivy was surprised and pleased to receive a text from Jaylen, inviting her to hang out in what was open of the Mystic Evermore Shopping Centre mall just after lunch.

Ivy answered in the affirmative, then did her mathematics homework before changing into her a stretchy top and jeans. Because she did not want to mess up her appearance walking, Estella gave her a lift into the center of town.

Ivy spied Jaylen sitting at one of the al-fresco tables in the courtyard between the shops. He was with Javier and Jeroma. She waved and Jaylen bounced towards her.

"Ivy it's great to see you," Jaylen said.

"You too," Ivy said. "Thanks for inviting me Jaylen."

"Let me get you a milkshake," Jaylen offered.

"Chocolate please," Ivy said.

Jaylen headed into the Milk Bar and Ivy settled down opposite Jaylen and Jeroma. "How are you guys this morning?"

"Good," and "Good," the Tilton siblings replied.

"You did say, chocolate?" Jaylen said returning with her milkshake. "So did you guys have fun with your games last night?"

"Oh yes," Jeroma said. "Netta had to kiss Javier!"

"Well just as long as no one kissed this one here," Jaylen said, looping his arm loosely around Ivy's shoulders.

Javier looked surprised and a little guilty. "I thought you were into Bridget Etheridge bud!" he said.

Jaylen laughed: "I'm over Bridget bud." He waved an arm dismissively. "Bridget is all yours, if you can fight Damien Nevermore for her."

"It was nice to see Wilson Booth last night though," Ivy said. "He was talking about trying to go and see Christy."

"It's a long way," Jaylen warned her thoughtlessly.

Ivy turned on him in surprise: "Do you know where Christy is?" she exclaimed.

"I have some idea, but I'm not supposed to say," Jaylen looked embarrassed.

"Would you take me?" Ivy spoke lightly, but her eyes were fixed on Jaylen with all seriousness. "Please Jaylen. I really want to see Christy!"

Jaylen went red. "Let me think about it," he said. "Of course, I would have to ask Carlice."

"Carlice - your ex?" Ivy exclaimed. Her lack of confidence fought with her desire to see Christy, and won out. There was no way Ivy was putting Jaylen into close communication with his beautiful, head-cheerleader ex-girlfriend. "Forget it!"

Jaylen eyed Ivy speculatively. "You know Carlice and I are just good friends? She really is in love with Fenton Etheridge."

"Yeah," Ivy admitted. "It's just I'm not ready to compete with her popularity."

"I think I have an idea," Jaylen said. "How would you like to go ten pin bowling this evening Ivy?"

"I would love it," Ivy said.

"Are you two in?" Jaylen asked Javier and Jeroma.

"I don't know," Javier said. "It looks as though you two want to be alone. I might go online and play my wizard in the role playing game."

"Thanks for asking me Jaylen, but I might read a book," Jeroma said.

The Tilton siblings finished their milk shakes and shared a bowl of curly potato fries. Then Javier and Jeroma set off for home on foot. Jaylen offered them a lift, but the Javier said that they would enjoy the walk.

Jaylen was left facing Ivy. "Do you want to get your coat before this evening?" he said. "It's almost the end of September."

"Ah yes," Ivy said. "If we could drop by my home - that would be handy."

The couple climbed into the four wheel drive, which had been parked at the rear of the mall. Jaylen started the engine, eased out of his parking space and drove through the car park. They turned north coming out of the city center and travelled through the fringes to Ivy's house.

"Do you want to come in?" Ivy invited Jaylen.

Jaylen shrugged. "I'm okay waiting here," he said.

That made sense, as Jaylen didn't need to meet her parents because they already knew each other through church. If Sunny had been home there would have been another male for Jaylen to talk to, but Ivy was sure her father was out in the fields, and only her stepmother was home.

Ivy used her key in the front door and walked softly through the corridors to avoid waking a sleepy baby brother. She reached her room and rummaged through her closet. If only she had a coat that would not reduce the style of her outfit! Jeans and a top were teen-age cool, but a coat was just bland. That is why she sometimes saw the fashionistas freezing to death in the mall for the sake of her looks. After some deliberation, Ivy decided to grab her lambs' wool lined long coat as it was tailored and fitted.

Ivy was almost back to the front door when her stepmother Estella appeared. "Where do you think you are going?" she demanded.

It was so unusual for Estella to play the stern parent, that Ivy jumped.

"Just out bowling with Jaylen," Ivy said.

"I thought you might be going much further," Estella said. "I know how much you have been missing your friend Christy."

"That is true," Ivy said.

"I suspected you might want to go and find Christy," Estella said. "And even that Jaylen might be able to help you. But I beg you to wait a while… Christy might be back sooner than you think, and she will never be the same."

"What do you mean?" Ivy demanded. Estella appeared to be talking nonsense.

"That terrible night of Christy's accident," Estella said. "I drove past the hospital and sensed that Christy had joined the cold ones."

"The cold ones?" Ivy exclaimed.

"Their hearts no longer beat and they will live forever, but not alive as we know it," Estella explained. "They are obliged to drink blood to stay active - your human legends call them vampires."

"I can't believe this!" Ivy exclaimed, although since discovering her stepmother was an alien, the improbable now seemed possible. Christy becoming a vampire would explain how strangely the Strahan family were behaving, and why no one knew exactly which hospital Christy was undergoing rehabilitation in. "How would Christy become a 'cold one'?"

"She must have died with vampire blood in her system" Estella said. "That is the only way."

"Those kinky love-rituals with Eduard Nevermore," Ivy said. "I told her they were gross – but now I understand."

"Please do not tell your grandmother," Estella said. "She does not believe in such things. She would say it was the devil."

"In a way she might be right," Ivy said. "Do you sense many more cold ones in this area Estella?"

"Less than there were before the Blackermores left," Ivy said. "But some far away, maybe more coming."

"Is Jaylen a cold one?" Ivy demanded in sudden alarm.

"No he has hot blood," Estella said. "Let him tell you all about it himself. You and he would have many beautiful puppies."

"The human word is 'babies'," Ivy said firmly, but a delightful picture of her and Jaylen playing with a littler of half-grown wolf cubs entered into her head and would not be dismissed. "Well, thank you for all the shocking information. I promise I will be careful, and

Jaylen and I really are only going bowling tonight. No visiting Christy, and no making puppies."

"Have fun then," Estella said, and left the room to do the washing up in the kitchen. "I have done my duty as your mother."

It was hardly a mother's way to deliver such shocking information as if it were everyday fact, and furthermore suggest that her step-daughter have puppies, but then again, Estella was new to the planet. Ivy shrugged and headed out of the door.

She climbed into the car next to Jaylen, who was indeed listening to the local radio. He looked up when she joined him: "The Sheriff and the men are planning to hunt that bear tomorrow afternoon," he said. "Some tracks have been spotted in woods on the Blackermore Estate."

"Are you planning to join the hunt?" Ivy inquired curiously. Jaylen was a strong young man and would likely be welcomed by the hunters.

"I don't know," Jaylen said. "I might just stay and protect you."

"Why would I be in danger?" Ivy asked.

"I dunno, but the estates run into the farming district and your house is on the fringe," Jaylen pulled up outside the Mystic Evermore Community Hall, which incorporated a bowling alley. "We are here."

They enjoyed a silly tea of chilly-cheese fries and hamburgers before attempting the bowling lanes. Jaylen was good at most things sporting, so accredited himself fairly well. It was one of Ivy's first times bowling, so she allowed Jaylen to coach her. Ivy also noticed that providing pointers on her game appeared to increase his confidence; so she played up her beginner status. The games that Jaylen bought were finished too quickly, and they hung around playing the arcade machines until eight o'clock.

"I guess I better take you home now," Jaylen said. "We didn't really give your parents a time."

"I don't think they will panic quite yet," Ivy said with a smile. However, her dad might be home now and she did always enjoy seeing him each Saturday night.

Jaylen drove sedately back to Ivy's house and parked in the driveway. He jumped out of the car and ran around to the other side to open the door for her. Then he walked her up to the front door and turned to face her. Ivy thought Jaylen was going to kiss her goodbye, but he didn't. Instead he looked serious.

"Ivy," Jaylen said. "If this is going to work, I have to tell you something."

He dropped down onto his hands and knees and began to strain as if he was stretching. However, nothing happened, except that Jaylen progressed through the yoga positions commonly referred to as angry cat and happy cat. He also looked particularly comical.

Ivy laughed. "I get it," she said. "You are a werewolf and you turn into a large dog whenever the moon is full."

"I somehow can't do it just to show you," Jaylen said. He was panting and red in the face from trying. "Not a week after the full moon and without Javier."

"I know you two are buds, but whatever does this have to do with Javier?" Ivy asked curiously.

Jaylen jumped up to his feet with an amazing show of strength and dexterity. "Javier is a wolf whisperer," he said. "With his help I can change anytime I want. I can also resist the full moon if need be."

"So he is your handler?" Ivy said.

"Of a sort," Jaylen said. "Javier thinks that in time I could control it on my own. But having him around has made my life much easier."

"I see," Ivy said. "Well as I had half worked this out, it makes no difference to me."

"I'm glad," Jaylen said.

"You were the dog that came to me and Estella in the forest and saved us from the bear weren't you?" Ivy said.

Jaylen hung his head. "Guilty."

"Don't be ashamed," Ivy said. "That was a beautiful thing to do." She reached up and kissed him on the cheek. "I will see you next time. Give me a call later."

"I will," Jaylen left the doorstep with a bounce in his step and half-bounded into his truck.

Ivy unlocked the house and stepped into the safety of its walls. It was one thing to suspect Jaylen was a werewolf, and dream about him being attracted to her, and quite another thing to have him admit it. She walked into the lounge room where her father was sorting through their DVD collection.

"Another horror movie Ivy?" Sunny inquired. "Or maybe science fiction?"

"I'm not in the mood tonight," Ivy replied. "Perhaps a comedy."

"A romantic comedy?" Sunny suggested.

Ivy grinned. "Knock yourself out!"

Her dad was one of the few guys who had a strong tolerance for chick flicks and could watch movies with his daughter all evening.

"I do love you Dad!" Ivy threw her arms around him and gave Sunny a big hug.

"It seems like you are in a loving mood all round," Sunny said. "Date go well?"

"Yes thanks," Ivy said. "That was my first date ever really, I wouldn't count double dating with Christy - the boys we went out with were always her pick."

"I am happy for you," Sunny said. "And the Mayor's son no less."

"You don't think I am reaching too high?" Ivy was concerned.

"Once maybe, but nowadays from what I hear, Jaylen is a very down to earth guy," Sunny said. "Just don't listen to his mother. The Pinkerton's own a fair slice of the land around here. The fact that I choose to till it with my own hands shouldn't go against my daughter."

"Oh Dad I know you are a solid guy," Ivy said. "What is Gran doing in the kitchen at this hour?"

"Baking scones for tomorrow," Sunny said. "The bear hunters and their wives all need to be fed you know."

****

Sunday after worship, Old Mrs. Pinkerton invited several of the ladies from the church to spend the afternoon at the Pinkerton house while their husbands were out on the bear hunt. They could have had their tea and sandwiches at the church hall, but Grandmother Pinkerton declared that visiting her house would be much more homely. The truth was, the Pinkerton house was the closest to where the housing estates bordered on the farm land and where the bear had been spotted, and the women wanted to feel they were involved.

Safely of course.

Ivy was enlisted on kitchen duty whether she wanted to help or not. There were sandwiches to cut and coffee to brew, and the church ladies always seemed to need a fresh cup. Estella graciously begged off hostess duties because she had to feed Liam and try to get him to sleep, despite the excitement of half-a-dozen church ladies cooing over him the minute before he was laid in his cot. Gran's scones were a great hit and were consumed while Ivy was preparing the first tray of sandwiches.

"It doesn't seem fair," Ivy moaned when Estella joined her in the kitchen to slice up apple to put on a fruit and cheese platter for the ladies. "Gran invites the ladies over, and my whole afternoon is slavery."

"Try not to think of it as slavery," Estella murmured. She slid a couple of notes into Ivy's hand. "Here is some extra pocket money for being so good and helping. I couldn't have managed entertaining the ladies by myself, with a baby to feed as well."

"Cool - thanks," Ivy cooed. She slipped the money into her apron pocket. It was a generous amount and she could see herself hitting the formal-wear shops in the mall to find something that would knock Jaylen's eyes out when he asked her to a dance or event. Not that she wanted him to go blind - that was just a saying.

"When can we go shopping?" Ivy asked.

"I will take you after school tomorrow if you like," Estella said.

"Tomorrow Jaylen has football practice," Ivy said.

"I expect Jaylen has a lot of football practices if you are going to be watching them all," Estella said teasingly. "Your father and I expect you to still get your homework done you know."

"I will have to juggle things carefully," Ivy said. "This is all so new to me."

Estella sighed. "Being in love is the most wonderful feeling in the world. Look at me and your father."

"Careful," Ivy warned. "You might begin to glow - and then the church ladies will conclude you are pregnant again."

"Do human women really glow when they are pregnant?" Estella inquired. "Melissa Nevermore looked quite dull the other day. Of course she had been injured."

"It's just a saying," Ivy explained. "I think it means they are healthy."

"With all that morning sickness?" Estella exclaimed.

"Yeah, even with all that morning sickness," Ivy had finished a plate of meat sandwiches, ready to follow the salad sandwiches she had delivered the previous round. She turned to carry it into the lounge, where the church ladies were gossiping and speculating about the bear hunt.

Estella followed carrying the fruit and cheese platter.

"Aren't you worried about your husband at the Farmer's Market today?" Old Mrs. Vaughn asked Estella. She was the mother of one of the senior firefighters who was participating, and was phenomenally proud of her son.

"The farmers still have to trade their produce," Estella said. "You wouldn't want the shops to be out of fresh fruit and vegetables this week would you?"

"Oh no dear," the old lady exclaimed. "But with the other men hunting the bear I would have thought..."

"We all help in any way we can," Estella replied patiently. "Ah yes dear we do," old Mrs. Vaughn rambled. "Including us women here, supporting our men."

Estella set the fruit platter down with a tight smile. The church women were well meaning, but they were not always NICE. "Help yourselves ladies."

Grandmother Strahan, who had been persuaded to leave the general store closed all day for once, gave Estella an understanding smile. "Thank you dear," she said.

"Estella is a good girl," Old Lady Pinkerton was heard to say as Ivy and Estella left the room. "I'm so glad that Sunny found her."

Ivy and Estella escaped to the kitchen and collapsed into uncontrollable laughter. It was that or take the old women's comments to heart and be hurt.

"The dear old things," Ivy whispered. "Eating all our sandwiches is such a great support for the men folk."

"Well at least the ladies are safe here, and not stressing too much," Estella said. "I am sure that was Grandmother Pinkerton's intention."

There was a tinkle of breaking glass in the back garden and Ivy and Estella ran to the kitchen window to look out.

"That sounded like Sunny's tomato frames," Estella cried.

"It is the bear," Ivy exclaimed, "In our back yard!"

There were squeals of excitement from the lounge and the grandmothers of Mystic Evermore Episcopalian Congregation all clustered unwisely against the French doors to the back yard to spectate. The movement caught the bear's eye and he roared, changing direction, and heading straight for the house.

"Get back," Estella screamed, but the grandmothers all panicked and clung together. At least they weren't screaming or moving.

The bear's eyes were pink and its eyesight appeared poor. It stopped and sniffed the air. The rear garbage bin caught its interest and the bear went and upended it, gobbling up some discarded cabbage leaves.

Estella used the momentary respite to usher the older women back into the lounge and shut the wooden door. Estella and Ivy continued to watch from the relative safety of the kitchen window.

The bear finished the edible contents of the bin and swallowed a few indigestible objects as well for good measure. Then it turned and shuffled towards the steps leading to the back porch where the family had often enjoyed their food in the open air.

Estella and Ivy shook in fear, doubting that the rear screens would really hold against a rabid bear.

There was a streak of grey, rust and white, and a canine body imposed itself between the bear and the back verandah. The dog barked and howled a challenge. The bear stopped, momentarily intimidated. The wolf planted his feet wide and fluffed his coat. He suddenly looked twice the size of a normal wolf.

Something came flying through the air and caught the bear around the neck. The bear stumbled and choked. Damien Nevermore and Jamie Lenore appeared from the woods, both running at superhuman speed. Jamie Lenore was carrying a nasty looking crossbow, the end of which had shot some sort of lasso around the bear's neck.

The men leapt over the fence, and with sublime disregard for any of Sunny's plants, grabbed the end of the wire that was hanging loose off the bear. It had some sort of handle attached so they could grip.

The bear rose on its hind legs and pawed the air, before clutching at its throat. Damien and Jaimie braced themselves and pulled on the lasso. A deadly game of tug-of-war commenced.

"They surely can't hope to win," Estella whispered. "The bear has the strength of ten men."

"Shush," Ivy whispered. "Watch."

Damien and Jamie held their end of the lasso tight and attempted to back away from the bear. If the bear had rushed toward them they would have been in trouble, but it attempted to bolt. It dragged Jamie and Damien for a few meters until it got tangled in the back fence.

The bear tore the fence out with a roar and continued in its path, but the wire now had a fencepost tangled in it as well as the two men pulling on it. The harder the bear pulled on the wire, the tighter the lasso closed around its neck. Finally it chocked itself.

Damien and Jamie sat down on the back lawn panting.

"That was a close one," Jamie exclaimed, before exchanging high fives and mutual slaps on the back with his companion.

"You are good, I will give you that!" Damien said. "But we owe it all to the dog - he got here first!"

"Where are you wolf?" Jamie called, but the wolf had melted into the shadows and run away into the wood.

"I hate sending him ahead to take the biggest risk," Damien observed, "But he is faster than both of us, and that is saying something."

Sunny Pinkerton came running from the Farmer's Market, which was closer than where the rest of the men had been left, all the way back on the Blackerwood Estate. Sunny grabbed a shot gun out of the shed and put a few bullets in the bear's skull just to make sure it did not revive.

"I saw you tearing through the market," Sunny explained. "Between you and the bear, half the stalls were knocked over."

"Lives were at stake," Damien said. "If the bear had got to the ladies - I don't want to say what would have happened."

"This bear has an unnatural interest in ladies, I must say," Sunny exclaimed. "And it's unnaturally big, even for a native bear. I would say someone had fed it growth hormone, like a farmer does a chicken."

"Amazing," Captain Etheridge exclaimed. He had just driven up in his army jeep. "You two beat me here and I broke the speed limit!"

"It's been tagged like a farm animal too," Sunny continued inspecting the bear. "Look in its ear. What does that tag say?"

Damien leaned close and pulled at the green cattle tag. "Nevermore," he read. "Do you know what this means?"

"The bear was a challenge," Captain Etheridge asserted. "The Blackermores are gone and Mystic Evermore is open to vampire wars!"

Damien spread his hands: "Let me count my troops. Three vampires - one vastly weakened by the death of the Mater, two witches - if they will cooperate, one werewolf, one wolf whisperer and one special ops army captain. It isn't much to hold a territory against other vampires with!"

"And one county Sheriff too," Sheriff Favor said, climbing out of her car. "I'm sorry I was late Damien. I care something for safety on the roads around here." She gave Captain Etheridge a stern look. 'You know you can always count on me Damien."

"Thank you Sarah," Damien said. He caught the sheriff's hand and bowed over it in a courtly gesture. The sheriff blushed.

"Get away with you Damien," Sarah Favor said. "Let's get back to business."

"You forgot about the hereditary vampire hunter," Jamie Lenore said. "My presence adds immensely to your strength."

"They don't know we are watching them," Estella whispered to Ivy. "Don't you think we should tell them we are here?"

"I guess so," Ivy said. She rapped on the window pane. "Hey boys - over here. And in the next room there are a bunch of frightened grandmothers. Is it alright to let them out?"

"I think so," Damien said. "Ask Sarah Favor. Now the emergency is over, we are reverting to the civilian authorities."

"I've always been in charge of the operation," Sheriff Favor scoffed. "Go ahead, get the ladies and assure them they are safe."

Ivy reflected that the way Sheriff Favor and Damien Nevermore looked at each other during moments of humorous exchange was very cute. In fact, it sort-of implied Bridget Etheridge ought to take herself out of the running for Damien Nevermore's attention. The Sheriff was a mature woman and surely would be able to compete in ways Bridget could not dream of at this stage.

The Mystic Evermore grandmothers were very grateful to hear that they had been saved from the rabid bear and that its carcass could no longer hurt them. Old Mrs. Pinkerton invited the conquering heroes into the house, where they sat down to relax, and more sandwiches were called for. This time old Mrs. Pinkerton joined Ivy in the kitchen to help prepare the refreshments.

Estella hugged Sunny. "I think you were just as brave as the other men," she said. "You were even in at the finish!"

"You cannot imagine how desperate I felt when I saw the men were chasing the bear in your direction," Sunny exclaimed. "Ivy, Liam, you and mother are all very precious to me."

Estella and Sunny did some kissing Ivy would have thought very cute if they had not been her parents. She also found herself longing for her first boyfriend and first kisses. Her mind went to the wolf that had faced down the bear to prevent it breaking into the Pinkerton house. The canine had disappeared immediately after the battle, but if that was Jaylen, it was the second time he had saved her life. She didn't think he got hurt this afternoon, but he easily could have been killed by the bear.

During a break from sandwich making, Ivy raced to her room and retrieved her mobile phone. She noticed it was blinking and indicating a message.

The message was from Jaylen. "Are you alright?" he had texted.

"Are YOU OK?" Ivy texted back.

"Yes," she got the reply. "I'm at Javier's."

"I'm so glad," Ivy texted. "You were so brave, but you left."

Ivy's phone rang. She pushed the green button.

"Well I could hardly perform a skin-change in front of the town grandmother's and whoever else you had in the house," Jaylen said.

"Did you see them?" Ivy was puzzled.

"Canine sense of smell," Jaylen said. "At least eight different people."

"You are right," Ivy said. "I've been wondering one thing. They say the bear was rabid. Can werewolves catch rabies?"

"I don't know," Jaylen said. "People can catch rabies though. I keep my shots up to date just in case."

Ivy giggled.

"What's so funny?" Jaylen asked.

"We are talking as if your condition was normal," Ivy said.

"It is normal for me," Jaylen said. "I need a girl who treats it as normal too."

"I would like to be that girl," Ivy ventured. It was unlike her to be so bold, but if she was reading Jaylen correctly, they were on the same page.

"I would like you to be that girl too," Jaylen said. "I had almost despaired of finding someone special."

"As the captain of the football team you could have anyone," Ivy suggested.

"Hero-worshipers like young Jeroma," Jaylen said. "Once I would have taken advantage, but nowadays I don't."

"I'm glad," Ivy said. "You seem much nicer than a couple of terms ago when you were going out with Carlice."

"I gave Carlice a hard time," Jaylen said. "I'm very sorry about that."

"Well she seems happy with Fenton now," Ivy said.

"Yeah," Jaylen said. "Did you know your step-mother smelled funny? Your little brother too."

"How funny?" Ivy asked.

"Sweet," Jaylen said. "They don't get as stinky as normal people."

"I had noticed Liam's nappies were remarkably tolerable," Ivy said. "How much do you remember from when you are the wolf?"

"Most bits," Jaylen said. "Although the wolf brain interprets things differently."

"Do you remember the capsule in the woods?" Ivy said. "Estella thinks that is her spaceship and she landed on earth a little over a year ago."

"Cool," Jaylen said. "Obviously you are keeping it quiet."

"Of course," Ivy said. "I can trust you."

"Yes," Jaylen said. "School tomorrow. Bye my sweet."

"Bye," Ivy said.

She put her phone on the charger and lay on her bed to dream nice waking dreams about herself and Jaylen. Let Grandmother Pinkerton take care of her own church ladies for the rest of the evening!

****

At school the next day, Ivy expected talk to be all about the bear hunt. However, the teenagers' attention moved along quickly. Mike Davis had reported seeing Christy Strahan back in town, apparently because she had dropped into the Snack Bar where he worked. Then she had been seen by someone's older brother at a licensed venue. Moreover, according to the older brother, Christy Strahan had come into the bar after dark, mincing on high heels and looking like a dominatrix.

"They say she was all 'hurt me now' in tight black leather," Mike reported. "With heavy makeup around her eyes and spiky boots up to her thighs. All she needed was a whip and handcuffs."

Ivy was somewhat shocked at Mike for talking like this because he was supposed to be a good church-going boy. The other boys of course were drooling. A few of them had always fancied Christy.

"It's not possible," Ivy said. "She was in rehab for treatment. She might not even be walking again yet."

"Oh trust me, Christy was walking," Mike laughed. "She looked like she might burst out of her hot-pants with every step, but she was walking. And drinking too."

"It's an offence to serve a minor," Ivy was doubly shocked.

"I didn't serve her alcohol," Mike said. "But she used fake I.D. to fool the staff member at the hotel who did serve her."

"If she was all sexy-like and had fake I.D. - how do you know it even was Christy?" Ivy inquired.

"I know it was Christy for sure," Mike said. "Why don't you ask Zarah if her sister is back?"

Zarah Strahan was almost as surprised as Ivy to hear that Christy had been spotted around town. However unlike Ivy, Zarah believed it might be possible Christy was walking again. Zarah explained that her sister's rehabilitation program had been more emotional than physical.

This did not fit at all with witness descriptions of Christy's accident, but then Ivy remembered that Estella sensed Christy had died and changed to become a 'cold one'. Perhaps incredible healing came with the vampirism.

"Is it safe?" Ivy whispered.

"I don't know," Zarah returned. "Christy was very angry. Mostly angry with Eduard Nevermore. If she has heard about him and Lena, she could be even worse."

"Oh-oh and she's here," Ivy whispered.

Christy Strahan strode into the senior locker area with an aura of power, and she was dressed pretty much as Mike had described. Click, click went her high heels on the stone floor; and strum, strum went the invisible air guitars through the campus speakers. Christy's top was leather and laced down the front. It gaped just enough to make every male on campus gawk at her front. Her leather mini-skirt hugged her hips and barely covered her underwear. Black stockings encased her legs and leather boots rose to above the knee.

Mr. Yore and Miss Byall considered giving Christy detention for her outfit, but postponed it till the morrow because they were so glad to see that she was apparently alive.

The bell rang for first period and Christy took no notice.

"Eduard Nevermore," Christy thundered. "You coward! Come and face me."

"I'm here," Eduard said, pushing himself to the front of the crowd. A bunch of students gathered around to spectate.

"You were a pathetic boyfriend," Christy continued. "Always moaning after your lost Lenore!"

"I'm not lost anymore," Lena said, unwisely joining Eduard in front of the group of students.

"Please stay out of this Lena," Eduard begged.

"Too late," Christy cried. "She is involved. Remember he only went back to you after I left!"

Christy reached out to Lena, and gave her a mighty push. Lena went hurtling across the locker area and would have fallen if Eduard hadn't moved with amazing speed to catch her. Christy then turned her back on Eduard and Lena and marched into the school cafeteria.

"I am ravenous," she declared.

The poor cook looked affronted. "I haven't begun preparing lunch yet," she cried.

"No matter," Christy declared. She snatched up a raw sausage and ate it straight.

Most of the students felt this was gross. A couple of boys managed to find it sexy.

"More," Christy demanded.

Eduard approached Christy, and Lena was no longer with him. Christy turned towards her former boyfriend and lover with a snarl. She spread her arms akimbo and braced her hands on her hips.

Dressed all in black she looked something like a crow.

"Nevermore," the angry girl snarled.

"I know you are mad at me," Eduard said. "But is this really a good idea Christy?"

"It is a great idea from where I stand," Christy said.

"Don't hurt Lena," Eduard begged. "It really isn't her fault."

"I have no intention of touching your beloved Lenore," Christy said. "I intend revenge on a larger scale." She raised her hand and displayed a large skull ring.

"Where did you get that?" Eduard asked. "It doesn't look like something of Booth manufacture."

"I was given it across the border in Tennessee," Christy said. "Where my loyalties now lie."

"Break it up please, students," Mr. Yore said. "First period is half over by now, and you all ought to be in your classes."

"Make me," Christy pouted.

Mr. Yore sighed patiently. "I don't see the point of your coming to school if you don't attend your classes Miss Strahan," he said peaceably.

Christy cocked her head. "You know what?" she said. "I think you are right. I'm going to all my classes and no one can stop me!"

"That's what you think," Eduard said hotly. He stepped towards Christy with a threatening stance, but Mr. Yore stopped him.

"Eduard Nevermore," Mr. Yore said sternly. "I have no desire to see you manhandle your ex-girlfriend. Go to the Principal's office at once."

"But Mr. Yore," Eduard began to object.

"Now Eduard!" Mr. Yore said. "Or I will be calling your older brother. In fact, I think that is a great idea. Ask the Principal to call Damien Nevermore at once!"

Eduard turned and walked doggedly towards the Principal's office, and Christy triumphantly continued her way toward the classroom.

Once she reached class, Christy sat down near the front and threw a gloating glance over her shoulder at Lena Lenore. It was obvious Christy thought she had made a point or won a battle. Lena shrugged and sat down.

Ivy somewhat nervously approached Christy. "May I sit here?" she inquired, indicating the seat next to Christy.

Christy looked surprised. Her gaze travelled over Ivy till it rested on the silver class ring she had distributed out earlier that year. It was rumored to be infused with verbena, which was thought to be protective. Ivy noticed that Christy no longer wore her own silver jewelry. She wondered whether it had been lost.

"I was sort-a saving the seat for Carlice," Christy said. "But I guess you can sit there."

"I was always your best friend," Ivy said, trying to disguise her hurt. "And I haven't heard from you for weeks."

"I know," Christy said. "Secrets and lies, secrets and lies - all necessary because of that dumb Eduard Nevermore."

"Boys," Ivy said, trying to infuse the right amount of scorn in her voice. "They are the source of all our troubles."

"By the way, I'm here if you need me," Jaylen said, boldly sitting in the desk just across the aisle from Ivy and Christy. He treated Ivy to an obvious wink.

Christy looked momentarily puzzled and then the light dawned in her eyes. "You and dog boy?" she asked Ivy.

"Maybe, I think so," Ivy was blushing.

Christy chuckled. "That's wild even for you!"

"A lot has changed," Ivy said. "Your accident rocked the world."

Christy looked pleased to hear that. "So I have been missed?"

Carlice slid into the seat next to Jaylen. "Hello Christy," she said.

"Hello Carlice," Christy said. "Thanks for everything. I know you and certain people did what you could."

"We wanted to help," Carlice said.

"Too bad it was not enough," Christy said. Her eyes became hard and angry again. "No one can give me back what I lost."

"I'm sorry," Carlice murmured. "Where are you staying?"

"In my grandmother's little unit," Christy said. "She doesn't need it because she's staying with my parents."

"Are you alright for school?" Carlice asked with veiled meaning.

Christy nodded. "I'm fine at school," she said. "It's just the Nevermores I hate - and my revenge will be huge."

"Damien didn't do anything bad to you," Carlice muttered.

"I know," Christy said. "But it doesn't make any difference. I hate him because of Eduard."

"I don't like to hear so much talk about hate," Ivy murmured.

Just then Mr. Yore entered the classroom and began to commence the lesson. History was late due to all the excitement, but better late than not at all. The students settled down and succumbed to the pressures of senior year school work, instead of the delights of gossip and schoolyard scandal.

Recess time Damien Nevermore approached Christy.

"Eduard has been sent home," Damien said. "And he will be kept out of school for as long as is necessary. I was wondering if I could have a chat with you."

"Oh sure," Christy said. She straightened up and became hard and sexy looking once again. Damien however, appeared immune to either her threat or her appeal.

Damien Nevermore and Christy Strahan strolled a few steps along the corridor, entered a vacant music room and faced each other. Ivy could see their profiles through the window. Damien's stance was authoritative, while Christy's was rebellious.

After a while Damien appeared to be soothing and calming, but when he extended his hand to Christy, she refused to shake it.

Damien then appeared nonchalant for a few minutes, before leaving the music room, shutting the door behind him and leaving Christy alone. Christy emerged from the room a few minutes later on her own and walked towards the locker area.

Damien turned to Jaylen and Carlice who had been hovering in the corridor.

"We have a problem," he said. "Follow me."

Damien headed towards the student car park, followed by Jaylen, Carlice, Ivy, and Javier. Fenton and Bridget Etheridge fell into step behind them. When they reached the car park, Damien leant against his car and faced his minions.

"I didn't really mean girlfriends and boyfriends too," Damien said.

"What does it matter?" Carlice said. "They know and they may be able to help."

"Okay," Damien said. "The long and the short of it is that Christy is so angry with Eduard that she has betrayed us to the vampires over the state-line in Tennessee. These vampires would have sensed the absence of the Blackermores, but they have been mobilized more quickly by Christy's report."

"I can't believe she would be so vindictive," Ivy exclaimed.

Damien looked resigned. "Christy has suffered a great loss," he said. "I can hardly blame her."

"But this will put her family and all the humans at risk, as well as us local vampires," Carlice exclaimed.

"Christy hasn't thought that far ahead," Damien observed.

"Perhaps we could tell her," Fenton suggested.

Damien shook his head. "I doubt she would listen," he said. "Fenton please contact your father, the Captain. Carlice, please call your mother, the Sheriff. We have until nightfall before the first wave arrives."

"And what should I do?" Zarah Strahan's voice sounded from behind the group facing Damien. She was accompanied by Jeroma Tilton, Paul Booth and Jamie Lenore, all from the junior class. "Christy is my sister."

"Zarah, you can warn your grandmother and your parents," Damien said. "Paul, please gather the Booth witches and attempt to throw a circle of protection around Mystic Evermore. Throw it as wide as you can sustain. Jamie, stick with me. The rest of you return to class for now."

The students pulled out their mobile phones and began notifying the people Damien required. Paul Booth headed off towards his home, as he was sure his father would understand, and phone the school back with permission for him to leave.

"Thank you," Damien said. "We are hardly ready for this battle, and one of the worst problems is what Christy could do from inside the territory. I would hate to restrain a locally born vampire, but it might be necessary."

"I have an idea," Ivy said. She remembered the way Wilson Booth had looked when he said that he would still like to find Christy and talk to her. "Let me go with Paul."

Ivy began to run to catch up to the African-American boy.

Jaylen caught her arm. "I will drive you," he said.

Ivy and Jaylen climbed into Jaylen's four wheel drive and passed Paul, who was leaving the school on foot. They pulled to a halt.

"Jump in," Ivy cried and Paul complied.

The four wheel drive rattled along the road until they reached the poorer part of town.

"You might have to guide me here," Jaylen said. "I only vaguely know the suburb where you live."

"Okay," Paul said, and with a couple of twists and turns, the vehicle pulled up in front of the Wilson house.

"Neater than I expected," Jaylen remarked.

Paul could have been insulted, but instead he treated the remark as a compliment. "My father was a homemaker and home handyman for years," he said. "Now he is a great caretaker for the council."

"I can see why they hired him," Jaylen remarked. "The paint trim, the doors and the fencing really stand out around here."

"Thanks," Paul said. He did not add that his father had to battle Jaylen's mother to obtain the position with the council. Jaylen had been more approachable at school in recent times, and most of the kids agreed he was not responsible for Mrs. Woodgate's snobbish acts.

Jaylen, Ivy and Paul entered the Booth house, where Paul introduced the teens to his father, and explained the emergency which required witchy assistance.

John Booth frowned. "As you know Paul," he said, "I burnt my powers out when I was young. I can only perform the simplest of magic with your help."

"But linked - we could throw a circle of protection," Paul objected. "For a distance?"

"Yes, but you are just developing your powers," John said. He sighed. "I have heard of your cousin Raven doing this sort of thing, but she is very independent. I don't know if she would join us."

"She is secretly dating Jamie Lenore," Paul said. "Surely if Jamie supports Damien, Raven would too?"

"Not necessarily," John remarked. "But we can ask her. And if she agrees, she is better set up than we are, so we had better go to her place."

John locked the house and everyone piled into Jaylen's vehicle and to drive the extra distance to the cottage Raven had inherited from Great-Grandmother Booth. Great-Grandmother Booth had been known as something of a New Age herbalist, so her cottage was on the outskirts. Raven also liked her privacy, so the isolation continued to suit her.

When they arrived at Raven's, they were relieved she appeared to be home. The cottage was quaint, but in need of some repairs and while there was a healthy herb garden around the back, the front garden was in need of weeding.

Seeing the direction of his father's gaze. Paul explained: "Raven has been alone since her great-grandmother died. There was no one to help her with repairs."

"I guess we would be the only family she has left now," John murmured thoughtfully.

"She barely knew of us when I first contacted her," Paul murmured. He strode up to the front door and touched the witch alarm. "That will bring her running," he chortled.

Sure enough, Raven's face appeared at the window in panic. "Oh it's you Paul!" she cried. "I wish you didn't think it was funny to do that!"

"My Dad is here too," Paul said.

"And Jaylen and Ivy I see," Raven said, recognizing her former classmates from school. Like Wilson Booth, Raven had struggled at school and dropped out for a while. Currently she was doing some online subjects at her own pace. "Come inside."

The witch alarm also sounded faintly when John Booth walked through the door.

Raven looked at him curiously. "You have powers, I see," she said. "But so faint."

"I burnt myself out binding the Mater Vampire in my youth," John explained.

Raven laughed bitterly. "I risk burning myself out all the time," she said. "But my powers just keep growing. So what brings you here?"

John looked serious, because he hated the thought of a witch using her powers so recklessly, but he did not dare criticize Raven. She was clearly far more capacious than John had ever been, and they needed her.

"We believe we will soon be under attack from vampires from Tennessee," Paul explained. "Damien Nevermore has asked us to throw a circle of protection around Mystic Evermore. We hoped you might help us."

"While I don't accept Damien Nevermore, or any vampire for that fact, as the local authority," Raven said, "I don't like the idea of an influx of rogue vampires any more than Damien does. I am with you."

"How large a circle can you throw?" Paul asked. "Could you cover the whole town?"

"Possibly," Raven said. "It would help if we could place some crystals around the perimeter to anchor it."

"I think we could drive around and do that," John said. "We have until nightfall."

"Couldn't the crystals be moved?" Paul inquired.

"Only from the inside," Raven replied. "We don't have any enemies in the town do we?"

"Unfortunately we do have one," Ivy said. She explained about the return of Christy Strahan and her role in the attack. "That's why I was looking for Wilson."

"What has Wilson got to do with it?" John Booth looked puzzled. "He is probably over at Strahan's right now anyway, because he works for Robbie Strahan's plumbing services."

"I can drop you off at the Strahan's, Ivy," Jaylen offered. "And we better go back to the Booth's and get John his own car so he and Paul can go out and set the crystals."

"Cool," Raven said. She retreated into a back room and returned carrying a box of assorted lumps of quartz. "Here you are, John and Paul. Lay these out at as regular intervals as possible."

"Is there a maximum distance required?" John asked.

Raven shook her head. "Less than a mile apart would be great, but to cover the whole town we might have to spread the anchors a bit thinner."

"Alright," John said. "Coming Paul? We will meet back at Raven's as soon as we can after we have finished."

The Booth father and son climbed back into Jaylen's all-wheel-drive along with Ivy, and Jaylen drove quickly and efficiently back to John Booth's house. Then Jaylen and Ivy continued on to the Strahan residence.

Jaylen parked the vehicle at the curb in the nearby street and they both got out. Ivy knocked on the Strahan's front door feeling a little shy. She really hadn't been around since Christy's accident.

It took Robbie Strahan a few minutes to answer the door because he didn't really run his plumbing business from the house, but the sheds out the back.

"Hello young Ivy," He said. "Jaylen Woodgate too. How can I help you today?"

"We are looking for Wilson Booth," Ivy said.

"Well Wilson is busy during work hours," Robbie said. "I sent him to unblock a toilet in the shopping mall. When he has finished there, he will probably drop by the Strahan General Store because Grandma wanted new taps in the pharmacy area."

"It is really important sir," Jaylen said. "We might wait for Wilson at the general store."

"After he is finished there he can leave for the day," Robbie said.

"Thanks," Ivy said.

Jaylen glanced at his watch nervously. "We better get moving Ivy," he said. "School will be out by now and there are only a couple of hours till the sun gets low."

"I assumed Damien meant six pm," Ivy said.

"In my experience," Jaylen said. "Vampires and other creatures can begin moving as the daylight decreases. One or two may cross the border before nightfall."

"Scouts do you mean?" Ivy inquired. "I thought they were waiting on a signal from Christy."

"I would be surprised if the interstate vampires trust Christy completely," Jaylen said. "Believe me, they will have a back-up plan in case we try to turn her to our side."

"Does that mean what we are trying to do is useless?" Ivy asked.

"No," Jaylen said. "One of our own who can give away all our secrets to the enemy is very dangerous. So let's go across the street to the general store."

The Strahan house was deliberately placed close to the Strahan General Store, because it was a family business and they wanted to be able to access it easily.

Grandma Strahan greeted the teens easily. "Hello Jaylen, hello Ivy, are you shopping to day?" Grandma Strahan said.

"No Grandma Strahan," Ivy said. "We are looking for Wilson."

"He is out the back," Grandma Strahan said. "I would appreciate it if you would wait a minute until he has finished."

"Oh of course Grandma Strahan," Jaylen said politely.

Ivy eyed the old lady who was well known as the town gossip. They said Grandma Strahan knew everything there was to know about Mystic Evermore. "Grandma, did you know Christy was back?" she asked.

"I had heard a couple reports from young men who saw her wearing some outrageous outfit in a nightclub," Grandma Strahan said. "However, the family weren't exactly expecting her yet."

"She came to school today," Ivy said. "Caused a great fuss. She said she was staying in your unit."

Grandma Strahan laughed. "So that's why my spare key moved," she said. "A little piece of advice. You kids take care around Christy. She hasn't been the same since her accident."

"We know exactly what you mean Grandma," Jaylen said. He raised an eyebrow at Ivy. Apparently the town grandmother was in the secret!

"Ah here is Wilson now," Grandma Strahan said. "Finished dear? Here are two of your old classmates to see you."

Wilson eyed Ivy and Jaylen speculatively. He had seen Ivy the previous weekend at the Davis house, but Jaylen had never really moved in the same circles as the Booths. "What do you want?" he asked.

"Could we go somewhere more private?" Ivy asked.

"I've got the plumber's van parked outside if that is suitable," Wilson suggested.

"Excellent," Ivy said.

"Will you two be okay if I leave?" Jaylen asked. "I need to find Javier and get ready to help Damien... with you know what."

"Of course," Ivy said. "Wilson and I are old friends."

Jaylen left and Wilson led the way to the Strahan plumbing van.

"What is it young Ivy?" he inquired.

"Do you remember what you said last Friday at the party?" Ivy queried. "About finding Christy and visiting her?"

"Yeah," Wilson said solidly. He crossed his arms across his body in a defiant stance and gazed at Ivy. "Did you want to go and find Christy?"

"That might not be necessary, because she is back in town," Ivy said. "But did you mean it - do you still care about Christy?"

"Of course I do," Wilson said stoutly.

"Even if she has - well - changed a bit since her accident?" Ivy asked.

"I assumed she had changed, that's what the rehabilitation was all about," Wilson said. "If you mean anything else, please be straight with me. I grew up in a Booth household and I know a bit of what happens around here in Mystic Evermore."

"Would you laugh if I said Christy had become a vampire?" Ivy ventured.

"No, I would not laugh," Wilson said. "Is it true?"

"Would it change how you felt about Christy?" Ivy asked.

"Slightly, possibly," Wilson said. "It would depend on how she was dealing with it, but I would still love her. That wouldn't change. It didn't even change when she chose Eduard Nevermore over me."

"Eduard is out of the picture, except that Christy now hates him and wants to get revenge upon the Nevermores for turning her into a vampire," Ivy said.

"I can understand that," Wilson said. "It's wrong, but understandable. She has lost her whole life as she knew it."

"I thought if you still loved Christy, you might be able to calm her down," Ivy said.

"It is worth a try," Wilson said. "Let's go find Christy."

"School is finished, so I don't know where she is now," Ivy admitted. "I had hoped to find you earlier - at your home."

"Okay," Wilson said. "Well if we can't use school to find Christy she might need to eat. Do you know where she would go for that?"

"You mean a restaurant?" Ivy asked.

"Think Ivy," Wilson said. "What do the vampires eat?"

"Blood," Ivy whispered. "But surely not our Christy."

"She won't be able to help her new nature," Wilson said. "If she is not snacking on people, what are the alternatives? The hospital for human blood supplies or the butcher for animal blood."

"She ate a raw sausage in the cafeteria," Ivy volunteered.

"The butcher it is then," Wilson said. "Quick before he goes home. Even if he is closing, he will let me in, I fix his sinks which get blocked fairly regularly."

The butcher was not far from the general store, although the shopping mall only housed the retail outlet, which was currently being managed by one of the assistants. Wilson checked the store briefly before continuing on to the industrial area, where the butcher had his slaughter yard and cold store.

The slaughter yard was clean and the methods used to stun the animals were as humane as possible, but there was no disguising this was a gory business. Ivy could see why a vampire might be attracted to the butcher's yard.

"Have you seen a young lady with black hair and tight leather clothing?" Wilson asked the butcher, giving the description Ivy had passed on to him. They had decided that it would seem more natural for him to inquire because he knew the butcher already.

"Yeah," the Butcher said. "I sold her a bag of offal and blood yesterday afternoon because she said she wanted to make her own blochwurst."

"Have you see her yet today?" Wilson inquired.

"Not yet," the Butcher said. "Although I've got her delivery all ready."

"Where were you taking that?" Wilson asked.

"Some address on the main drag," the Butcher said.

"Grandma Strahan's unit," Wilson said, checking the slip of paper briefly. "We are going in circles." He pulled out his wallet. "I tell you what, I will pay you for the bag of blood and take it to the young lady."

"Suits me," the Butcher said. "I get my money and one less delivery to make. Here it is, all packed in ice to keep it safe and cool."

Some money exchanged hands and Wilson stowed the cool box safely in the rear of the van.

"Now we have Christy's tea," he said. "We will just go back to her house and wait."

Wilson threw the van into gear and headed back towards the main drag.

"I cannot believe you are so calm about this," Ivy said.

"I see worse sometimes at work," Wilson said. "And if I'm serious about Christy, I cannot afford to be squeamish about her needs."

"At least we are prepared, so she won't snack on us," Ivy said, but it didn't really feel like a joke. "Wilson are you scared?"

"A little," Wilson admitted. "But not worse than the first time I tried to ask Christy out."

"What happened?" Ivy asked.

"She gave me the 'just good friends' speech," Wilson said. "It broke my heart."

Ivy reached out and squeezed Wilson's hand sympathetically where it rested upon the steering wheel. The naturally defensive boy allowed the hand to remain. There were tears gathering in Wilson's eyes. He had obviously been strongly affected by Christy's rejection.

"Not you two as well," a voice sounded from behind Ivy. "I thought I went through enough with Lena and Eduard." It was Christy.

Ivy moved her hand off of Wilson's quickly. "Christy, I am with Jaylen," she said. "Wilson and I are here because we both care about you."

"It sure looks like it when you are sitting there holding hands," Christy snapped.

"I know everything Christy and I still love you," Wilson said. He climbed out of the truck and approached Christy, sliding his arms around her. He bowed his head and bared his neck to her just below the ear, making himself completely vulnerable.

Christy flinched and jumped away. "Please don't tempt me," she said. "I have heard that if I kill a human, Jamie Lenore will execute me. I don't want to run afoul of the hereditary hunter."

"Perhaps this will help," Ivy said, climbing out of the van with the cool box containing the animal blood.

"Oh wow," Christy said. "You are a lifesaver, and you do really understand." She pulled out the keys to her grandmother's flat. "We can't do this outside, please come in."

Christy unlocked the front door, and Ivy and Wilson followed the vampire into her lair.

"Gran has some soft drink," Christy offered. "It is no good to me, although I can appear to drink it."

"We would love soft drink," Ivy said. "While you have yours."

"I don't usually pour it into a glass," Christy admitted. "But I guess I better learn to be civilized."

"Christy," Ivy began. "I need to talk to you about something. There is a rumor going around that you have invited the interstate vampires into this territory."

"The Tennessee vampires are very nice," Christy said. "Carlice took me to them so that they could help me learn to control my vampire urges. And they even gave me this ring. She looked at Wilson somewhat accusingly. "Raven Booth wouldn't make me a daylight ring."

"Please don't hold it against me Christy," Wilson said. "Raven is only a distant cousin of mine, and a law to herself."

"Perhaps," Christy admitted. She took a long draught of her lamb's blood. "This is so revitalizing. I wish I didn't need it, but I do."

"We understand Christy," Ivy said. "But I need you to understand too. With only four vampires in town, your human friends and family are much safer. The interstate vampires are bringing rogue vampires with them. People will get hurt."

"The Tennessee vampires wouldn't bring rogue vampires here," Christy said. "They hate rogues as much as the Blackermores did."

"They might not have a large enough army without the rogues," Ivy explained. "There are hundreds of rogue vampires camped out on our borders just waiting."

"Damien Nevermore is pretty powerful," Wilson added. "I haven't heard the full story, but logic tells me that anything that can defeat Damien Nevermore has to be bigger and badder than him. We don't want that here!"

"Well with only four vampires in town, who would I date?" Christy cried. "And don't say either of the Nevermore brothers - that would make me sick."

"If you would consider dating a human," Wilson said, "You could date me. Or aren't I bad-boy enough for you nowadays?"

"I didn't know that side of Eduard. Wilson you were always very sweet and I didn't value you enough," Christy said. "I did think about you after my accident, but I thought you would never be able to accept me."

"There are miracles as well as tragedies around Mystic Evermore," Wilson said.

"So I am learning," Christy said. She stood facing Wilson and cupped both of his hands in hers. "Wilson Booth, will you kiss me?"

"I surely will," Wilson breathed, "If you would mind cleaning your teeth a little first?"

Christy blushed. "I forgot I was just drinking blood." she said. She retreated into the bathroom momentarily and emerged smelling of mint.

Wilson slid his arms around Christy. Christy reciprocated and reached up to loop her arms around Wilson's neck. Their lips met in a kiss that appeared mutually satisfying as they did not emerge until Ivy was thoroughly embarrassed from trying not to watch them.

"I think I had better get going," Ivy stammered. "I can see myself out the front door."

"Okay Ivy," Christy said. "Thanks for everything. And you can tell Damien Nevermore that I won't be giving the signal for the interstate vampires to begin the attack."

"Cool, thanks Christy," Ivy said. Ivy opened Grandma Strahan's front door and stepped out. It was the kind that would lock behind her if she pulled it closed.

Ivy stood on the main street of Mystic Evermore, a few blocks before the mall, and at least half an hour's walk from home. A supernatural battle for the territory was brewing and dusk was falling. It was not a good time for a girl to be out alone.

Ivy's phone beeped and she checked it to find an area-wide text message from Sheriff Favor. The Sheriff had called a curfew. All citizens were to retreat to their own homes and lock the doors and windows.

Any citizens who had silver weapons, like the silver pronged forks that had been distributed for the rat hunt, were to keep them handy. The Sheriff hoped that the risk was small, but a gang of ruffians had been spotted loitering around town.

"It would be nice to be inside," Ivy whispered to herself, considering whether to make for her own home or simply knock on the door of Christy's parents' house, which was far closer. Grandma Strahan had locked the shop, and that building was all dark.

Ivy felt something furry under her hand and glanced down. It was the wolf, glinting silver and with brown and grey flacks in the dusky light.

"Oh Jaylen," she exclaimed. "Thanks for coming back for me."

The wolf snuffled at Ivy's hand, as if he could not get enough of her scent.

"Do you want me to come with you?" she asked. "I forgot, I have a message for Damien Nevermore."

The wolf yapped, its call being sharper than that of a normal dog.

"I don't know whether you understand me," Ivy said. "But it's a long walk either to home or Nevermore Manner if that is where Damien is organizing his defense."

The wolf squatted down on the ground and slowly lowered its shoulders down as well as its haunches.

"I said walk - not sit," Ivy began, but then paused. The wolf seemed to have grown, and even sitting, its back reached past her knees. "Do you want me to climb on your back?"

The wolf panted and licked at Ivy with its wild wet tongue, and generally looked impatient. Ivy climbed onto its back and flung her arms around its neck. She could have held onto the shaggy coat, but she did not want to pull his hair.

The wolf rose to its feet, feeling solid and sturdy under Ivy. Then it began to run, the bouncing action causing Ivy to cling on for dear life. Half-an-hour on foot became less than five minutes riding on the wolf and they were soon loping up the driveway of Nevermore Manner.

Ivy slid off Jaylen-wolf's back and knocked on the imposing front door. Eduard Nevermore opened the door. "Come in quickly," he exclaimed. "We are all preparing for the battle."

"I have good news," Ivy said. "Christy is commencing a relationship with Wilson Booth and has promised not to give the signal for the war to begin."

Eduard looked serious, and far more like the hundred-year-old vampire Ivy now knew him to be, than the teenage boy she was used to seeing at school.

"While I am personally thrilled to hear Christy has moved on, I'm afraid the lack of signal might only confuse the enemy and buy us a little time," he said. "Half an hour to an hour, or two hours if we are really lucky! However, there is a huge army on our fringes. They will not simply go away without attacking."

"I guess that makes sense," Ivy said, although she was bitterly disappointed her brilliant idea had helped so little.

"It will be a long night," Eduard said, leading the way from the front door to the main living area of Nevermore Manner. "The witches have set up in the dining room, as we decided the Manor was more defensible than Raven's little cottage."

"Good thinking," Ivy said.

"Sebastian and Melissa have retreated to the cellar," Eduard said. "There is a bunker down below and it is completely impenetrable when sealed from the inside. It is very important to protect the human owner of all the land."

"Interesting," Ivy said. Normally Uncle Nevermore and Melissa had their own cute little cottage in town, a symbol of how integrated they were with the local folks. However, since the bear attack, they must have become nervous. "I hope Melissa is feeling better."

"Much better," Eduard said. "There is a nurse with her to give administer her antibiotics and painkillers, and change her dressings, but she has been released from hospital."

"Gran would be happy to hear that," Ivy said.

"The rest of us are in the main lounge discussing our roles in the upcoming battle," Eduard said. "You had better join the friends and girlfriends in whatever they do."

"I would like to be with Jaylen," Ivy whispered, patting the wolf who was walking by her side.

Eduard shook his head. "Jaylen has been out scouting for unprotected humans, and making sure they retreat indoors, to lock themselves inside as the Sheriff ordered. Even if it is for fear of a big wild wolf! In a few minutes, he will be sent out to search for enemy vampires who have sneaked across the border before it was sealed."

"That sounds dangerous," Ivy stammered. She clutched at the wolf's shaggy fur.

"He won't be alone," Eduard said. "Captain Etheridge will be going with him, and possibly Damien or Jamie, it is all under discussion. Damien being our king piece, so as to speak, we aren't sure whether to hoard him or deploy him."

"I think I will leave the strategy up to you guys," Ivy said. "It's all a little overwhelming."

Eduard laid his hand on the lounge room door, "Here we are," he said.

Eduard opened the lounge room door and Ivy quickly ran her eyes over the assortment of local people in the room. There were the known vampires - Carlice Favor and Damien Nevermore. Ivy was beginning to understand that Javier Tilton played some sort of role, apparently complimentary to Jaylen's wolf.

Captain Etheridge and the Sheriff were obviously in the intelligence loop regarding the secrets of Mystic Evermore. Jamie Lenore was lounging across a chair, his form appearing impossibly muscle bound and even more sinewy than when he was at school. A couple of other kids who were close to the Nevermores were sitting anxiously beside their friends and partners.

Then Ivy gasped in shock because she saw her stepmother, Estella standing directly opposite Damien Nevermore, apparently deep in conversation with him. As Ivy moved closer, Estella seemed to be giving a count of the opposing army, the best she could using her extra-terrestrial senses.

"Estella - mother!" Ivy cried.

Estella stopped what she was doing and ran towards Ivy. "Ivy dear, I have been so worried!"

"Whatever are you doing here?" Ivy inquired.

"I was driving around Mystic Evermore looking for you on the streets because you had not returned home after school," Ivy said.

"Then I met Eduard Nevermore and he directed me to come to the Manor. He said you would be here eventually."

"I'm so sorry," Ivy admitted. "I forgot to even text you or Dad."

"In these days of mobile telephones there is little excuse," Estella admonished sternly.

"So how come you have revealed your nature?" Ivy said. "I thought we were keeping things quiet."

"I could sense things on the border that I really do not want entering Mystic Evermore," Estella explained. "And these people here, they all keep each other's secrets."

"I see," Ivy said. "Where is Liam?"

"In the next room with the witches," Estella said. "Neither Liam nor I have any offensive powers that I know about, but the witches found they could sustain a stronger circle with his carry-cot in the center than without. He is like a little battery for their power."

"I hope he doesn't get hurt," Ivy said.

"So do I," Estella Exclaimed. "I hope none of us get hurt... and I will be joining the witches too when it is time - which will be very soon!"

"Do you think Grandma will be alright without us?" Ivy asked anxiously.

"Your father will protect her, and they should be okay if they obey the Sheriff's instructions and stay inside," Estella said. "He won't be out looking for me because I told him I was safe here."

"I bet he was surprised," Ivy laughed. Estella was normally such a good, stay-at-home wife.

"You need to say goodbye to Jaylen now," Damien said to Ivy. "He and Captain Etheridge are about to go back on patrol."

Ivy looked around for the wolf, as Jaylen's furry presence was no longer directly under her fingertips. She found him lavishly licking Jeroma Tilton, who was hugging and kissing him effusively. Ivy added her hugs to Jeroma's, feeling glad that the pair were slightly less effusive when Jaylen was in his human form. Ivy kissed Jaylen on the top of his head, feeling strange that their first real kiss should be when he was in wolf form.

"Be safe," Ivy whispered.

Jeroma clutched Ivy's hand as they watched Jaylen and the Captain exit the Manor. "Jaylen is so brave," Jeroma whispered. "Did you hear about the time he saved my life?"

"I'm not sure," Ivy returned. "But he has saved my life several times so far."

"It is past nightfall," Damien Nevermore said. "Let us go to the witches and ask them to make the boundary permeable so that Jamie can go out and hunt."

Jamie Lenore stood up. He was wearing multiple quivers full of silver tipped arrows, and had bags of garden stakes strapped to his back. His crossbow was held in one hand, and his sword was strapped to his side. If either of those failed, he had throwing knives inserted to a webbing of belts and a small cutlass tucked away as well. The sight was indeed impressive.

Jamie shook Damien and Eduard by the hand. "Give me a few minutes to reach the barrier," he said, and exited the Manor by the main door. Two of the Sheriff's most trusted men slammed it shut behind him.

Damien crossed the hallway, and entered the dining room where Paul and John Booth had formed a triangle of power with Raven as the focal point. Liam's little carry-cot was parked in the center of the triangle and he was glowing a comfortable yellow. All seemed to be going well with the protection casting.

"Jamie is on his way to the boundary," Damien instructed. "Please let him through."

Estella traced the path she sensed Jamie was following on the map. "Weaken the boundary just here," she suggested.

Raven concentrated and the yellow glow above Liam flickered momentarily.

"He is through," Estella whispered.

Raven increased the protection spell and the yellow glow steadied. "Did anyone go with Jamie?" the Witch asked. "Captain Etheridge perhaps?"

Damien shook his head: "Jamie said he wanted to set a new record for the number of hereditary hunter kills in one hour."

"You sent him alone?" Raven was angry. "There must be a thousand rogue vampires out there."

Raven broke out of the protection triangle, and everyone in the room cried out in fear and alarm. "The protection!"

Strangely the protection did not fail despite the absence of its most powerful caster. Estella simply reached out and smoothly took hold of the threads, and after a brief second of weakness, the yellow glow was as steady as ever.

"I cannot cast a spell," Estella said, "But now it is cast, and since it is pure protection, which is good, I can hold it for as long as is required. Until morning even! You can go and join your man, Raven girl."

Raven gave Damien Nevermore a hard look. "You haven't heard the last of this," she shouted before disappearing in a puff of smoke.

"Jamie was born to kill vampires," Damien observed. "I'm pretty sure he would have been okay. However, having Raven out there throwing balls of fire around too won't hurt. Do you know how to let them in again when they ask Estella?"

Estella nodded. "Jamie has his locator rune," she said. "I can also feel rogue vampires dying or running away from the hunter."

"If we are lucky, that is mostly what they brought," Damien said. "But I do need to hatch a plan to deal with any vampire aristocracy that may be leading the attack."

Ivy watched Estella holding the protection spell for a few minutes. Her stepmother appeared perfectly comfortable where Raven had sweated and strained. The power Raven had gathered flowed steadily through Estella from Paul, who was now manipulating it, back to John who was helping in his small way. Estella appeared to function as the filter, while Liam was the battery for the magical system.

After about an hour, Estella reported a tugging sensation at a point in the barrier, and Paul manipulated the force to allow Jamie to return to the protected area. He was holding Raven by the hand when they reappeared. Both were dirty and sweaty, but neither appeared injured.

"Four hundred killed," Jamie reported. "That is around a kill a minute. I've never had so much fun in my life."

"Three hundred kills of my own," Raven announced.

"You do cheat by killing a number at once with those scattering fireballs," Jamie remarked.

"It's not cheating and you needed me," Raven asserted. She frowned at Damien Nevermore. "I still haven't forgiven you for sending him out alone."

"I would have loved to have gone with him," Damien said. "But that might have opened Mystic Evermore up to occupation. It isn't all fun and games being the strongest vampire in town. I actually miss the Blackermores!"

Raven scoffed. "Sure Damien."

"There are good pickings out there still," Jamie remarked. "I would like a cool drink, and several more quivers of arrows before I go back. I do hate wasting my knives, and it was so much fun to appear and surprise them all, that I thought I would do it again."

"Estella, I need you on intelligence duty, if Raven could rejoin the protection circle," Damien instructed.

"I need a cool drink too and then I will help you Damien," Raven said. "So long as you don't plan to send Jamie out alone again."

"This time I will go with him," Damien said. "I can't allow Jamie to have all the fun on his own. Eduard will be vampire-in-charge inside Mystic Evermore, and you will have Sheriff Forbes too."

"I was fine," Jamie muttered. "Luckily Captain Etheridge's rules appear to contain an exception for times of war. I so rarely get to kill a vampire lately."

"Well, you will have your fill of killing tonight," Damien said, "Even if Captain Etheridge's rules resume tomorrow."

Jamie rested for about half an hour and drank several liters of water to rehydrate. Then he kitted up with several more sheaths of silver tipped arrows, and sacks of garden stakes. Damien also armed himself with a great sword for swiping heads off vampires, and a stack of stakes.

Then the two fighters exited the Manor and set out for the border on foot. Apparently the locator rune could help bring the holder directly back, but could not send them out again. Estella nodded when she sensed they had reached the perimeter.

Raven concentrated and the protection glow wavered briefly. Out in the field, Damien and Jamie slipped through the protection and appeared amongst the enemy army. They began killing lesser vampires at once. Raven strengthened the protection circle and the rogue vampires outside its circumference beat upon the barrier futilely in an attempt to gain entry.

All was calm in Nevermore Manor while the battle raged outside its borders, until Estella gave a cry.

"I can sense a cold one, very old and powerful," she said.

"Where is it?" Eduard asked anxiously.

"Inside the barrier," Estella wailed. "Coming towards the Manor."

Raven was covered in sweat, and shaking from her efforts to hold the protection circle against the creature. "It is true," she said. "With Damien outside the circle, it became much harder to withstand the powerful vampires outside."

"Call Damien back," Eduard ordered.

"That is easier said than done," Raven exclaimed. "The locator rune activates from their side, not ours."

"Damien won't risk staying outside the circle for too long," Eduard said. "He will come back of his own accord."

"What about Jaylen and Captain Etheridge?" Ivy asked anxiously.

"Patrolling in a different part of the territory just now," Estella said. "The cold one will reach us before they do."

Eduard gave orders quickly. The Sheriff's men were all armed with silver bulleted guns and stakes, and positioned in the outer rooms of the Manor with orders to shoot on sight. Carlice was to stay by his side and add to his vampire powers if possible.

Moments later, there was a thunderous knocking at the front gate. A voice sounded clearly in the house without the assistance of any amplification.

"Eduard Nevermore," the Uber Vampire called, "It's Andy Jackson here, let me in."

Eduard was over a hundred years old, but the vampire calling to him was a century older. Eduard could hardly resist its instructions. He trembled and caught hold of a nearby doorframe to stop himself from automatically obeying. Carlice grabbed him around the waist and also tried to hold him back.

"Block your ears everyone," Eduard instructed. The Sheriff's men put their earmuffs on, and the rest of the occupants of the Manor put their fingers in their ears. Except Carlice who was holding Eduard, and the witches who were mostly immune to the vampire's charisma.

"Eduard Nevermore," Jackson called again. "I know your brother is not here - he is out on the battle field. You are weak and pathetic, and you must obey me. Let me in!"

Eduard could no longer resist, he began the journey out the front door and down to the gate, with Carlice dragging behind him at every step.

"Please, no!" Eduard cried.

The Uber Vampire calling himself Jackson chuckled.

"Cease!" It was Javier Tilton, striding down the hallway and out onto the porch steps, with his black coat flying behind him, and the heels of his boots clicking. His voice was almost as full of command as that of the Uber Vampire.

Eduard froze on the spot.

Jackson sounded confused. "Who or what are you?"

"I am Javier," Javier replied. "Javier said with a 'J'." He deliberately omitted his last name to show the Uber Vampire that he was not affected by any compulsion to answer. "I am a wolf whisperer."

"A wolf whisperer," Andy Jackson sounded thoughtful. "How rare and valuable an asset for the area. But you have no power over me."

"That is true," Javier replied. "The most I can do is calm you down. But then you won't want to fight the Nevermores anymore. You will want to go away in peace."

"It is right I am beginning to feel calm," Jackson replied. "Perhaps it is safe for you to let me inside the compound."

Javier laughed. "A trick!" he exclaimed. "I cannot let you in until Damien returns - and even then, it will be his decision."

"I see you are a wise boy," Jackson said. "I say boy, because I sense you are young. If you came to work for me, I would give you many rewards."

"I just want to finish school and maybe find a girlfriend," Javier said. "My needs are very simple."

"All the girls in the region could be yours," Jackson continued.

Javier laughed. "What would I do with so many girls?" he asked. "I take care not to whisper the ones I know into liking me anyway. I want to be liked naturally."

"And how is that going for you?" Jackson inquired conversationally.

"Not so good," Javier said. "But I have no intention of allowing you to distract me with small talk."

"I will bash this gate down," Jackson finally announced in frustration.

"Just you try," Javier said. "See what happens."

Javier adopted an intense look of concentration, and his opponent sighed. The wolf whisperer was indeed persuasive.

"Suddenly I'm not in the mood," Andy Jackson admitted. "I'm feeling very relaxed."

"It's been a busy evening," Javier remarked. "Perhaps you want to go to sleep."

"I am feeling very sleepy," Jackson yawned. There was a soft thud outside the gate. It sounded as though a heavy body had slumped to the ground.

"Well done Javier," Damien Nevermore said, appearing suddenly in the hall behind Javier. "I couldn't have done better myself. In fact, I'm not sure I could have even done that!"

Damien had been transported home by the locator rune. He walked out onto the porch followed by several of the Sheriff's men. The police officers were equipped with silver handcuffs and long chains. They looked relieved to be accompanied by Damien.

"Open the gate now," Damien ordered. "Be very careful in case the Uber Vampire is not really asleep and is just feigning."

"Such power," Javier murmured. "I have never felt anything like him. Of course, I never confronted either of the Blackermores."

"There are older vampires than Jackson in the world," Damien said. "And we have to convince them all to leave Mystic Evermore alone."

The police officers opened the gate and stepped carefully outside, their silver loaded guns cocked. A couple of rogue vampires who had accompanied their leader attempted to scramble away, but the policemen shot them through the heart with deadly aim. The vampire bodies slumped, and as they fell, crumbled into piles of dust.

Damien stepped outside as well. "You know what to do guys," he said.

The police carefully handcuffed the Uber Vampire using multiple silver handcuffs for both his wrists and ankles. Then they draped him with silver chains. After adding all that weight, it took six of them to carry the sleeping Uber Vampire inside, where they chained him to a silver infused metal chair.

"Wake him up," Damien ordered, and the police threw several buckets of cold water on the Uber Vampire, only pausing when it stirred.

"Where is Sheriff Favor?" Ivy inquired curiously.

"Down in the cellar with Uncle and Melissa," Damien murmured almost tenderly. "She thinks she is on guard duty, but in reality, Sarah Favor is far too precious to risk losing in a battle like this."

Ivy thought that Bridget Etheridge, who had not been safe-guarded in the cellar, but allowed to remain upstairs amongst the other human connections and friends, got a funny look on her face at this statement. Bridget and Damien were officially broken up, but rumor had it that Bridget still believed herself to be the main woman in Damien Nevermore's life. Perhaps she had just had a wake-up call that would allow her to consider other romantic partners.

"Damien Nevermore," Jackson muttered drowsily. "You are back."

"I am," Damien said firmly. "What does this attack on my territory mean?"

"It is not your territory," Jackson said. "It is the Blackermores' territory. And we had reports they were absent and their subjects dissatisfied with your rule."

"You thought there was vacant land and plenty of human victims more likely," Damien said. "I am the Blackermores' closest relative and a direct descendant of Henrietta Ermore. I need you to acknowledge me leader of this area."

Even chained, the Uber Vampire called Jackson looked imposing. He scoffed. "I could only ever accept you as an equal - if even that," he said.

"That would be good enough for me," Damien said. "Acknowledge me as an equal and return to Tennessee."

"Much as it pains me, I might just have to do that!" Jackson said. "Although you may not be an ancient vampire, you do not fight alone. Tell me, how do you get the hunter to fight by your side? The witches to cast spells for you, and this whisperer to support your rule? The human authorities even, to do your bidding?"

"I achieve that by living in harmony with the humans in my area," Damien replied. "You could try it in your area and see what happens."

"What then would we eat?" the Uber Vampire calling himself Jackson inquired.

"There are animals," Damien said. "Specially bred farm animals can be very tasty."

"And do you never taste human blood to increase your strength?" Jackson queried.

"Occasionally someone volunteers," Damien admitted. "Although biting a human becomes much more personal when it is done with their consent."

"It does sound appealing," Jackson said. "I must say I do enjoy the flavor of infatuation."

"You should try love," Damien said. "It is much nicer and even more of a delicacy."

"I don't know if I can love again after all these years," Jackson admitted. "But I may open myself to the possibility."

"Back off a bit Javier," Damien requested. "I need to be sure this agreement is for real and not part of your influence."

"I'm not doing anything," Javier protested, but he left the room.

The Uber Vampire continued to regard Damien calmly. "Truly Nevermore, you have proved yourself," he said. "All I need now is to be re-united with what is left of my army, and allowed to return to my territory."

155

"I would feel a bit safer if you and your army actually departed in different directions," Damien observed wisely.

"If that is the gesture of goodwill that you require, I will dismiss my army and send them to the east while I continue to the north," Jackson suggested. He withdrew the large daylight ring he was wearing on his finger. Only elite witches knew how to manufacture such rings, and not all ancient vampires even had them.

Jackson held the ring out to Damien. "Brother, I surrender my ring to you, so that you know I will not turn directly around and attack you again. You can have it messengered to me once I am in my home at Nashville."

"Very good," Damien said.

He instructed the police officers to carry the Uber Vampire to one of the vehicles and lay him down in the back seat, and then they set out for the edge of Mystic Evermore. The witches dropped the protection spell briefly when they received Damien's text advising them that his party was at the protective border.

A few minutes later, Estella nodded as she sensed the group of rogue vampires was scattering towards the east. A few individuals had already deserted and progressed in other directions. True to his word, Jackson himself was travelling directly to the north.

"The Tennessee vampires will have to hurry if they wish to reach some sort of shelter before day-break," Eduard remarked. He slumped into a chair. "That was exhausting."

"Poor Eduard, you have not fully recovered from your illness yet," Lena gushed, and began to fuss over him.

The crunch of wheels upon the gravel driveway indicated the return of Damien Nevermore and the Sheriff's men. They had turned towards the Manor as soon as the enemy vampires had dispersed.

Damien was twirling Jackson's daylight ring between his fingers thoughtfully. "Beautiful work," the young man exclaimed, and passed it to Eduard.

Eduard inspected the day ring that the Uber Vampire had left behind as surety. It was indeed nicely made. "This is very valuable - why don't we keep it as spoils of our victory?"

"I want to grow a reputation for honorable dealing amongst the rest of the vampire community," Damien said. "Returning the ring as promised will be a start." Damien hesitated: "This is why perhaps I am lead vampire and not you."

Eduard shrugged. "I don't envy you the post - but I will have you know that I have always done what I believed to be right."

"I understand that you have," Damien observed. "Yet you also judged everyone else – and that sort of narrow morality can be very dangerous."

"It is very natural though," Eduard said. "Which is one reason I don't understand why I got sicker than you when the Mater Vampire was killed."

"We may never know!" Damien said, "Cheer up brother, you will regain your strength!"

"I hope so," Eduard said. "Being compelled by that vampire was very humiliating. Even Carlice had better resistance!"

"Try to forget it, now the threat is over," Damien said.

The elder Nevermore strode into the dining room. "Estella," he asked, "Do you think it is safe to drop the protection circle and give the witches a rest?"

"Well there are a few confused vampires circling around aimlessly," Estella said. "If we drop the circle they may enter."

"I think we can clean them up from within our territory if they do enter," Damien observed. "I am mindful that your infant is in the center of the circle and it has been a long time since he was fed."

"Liam looks well enough, but thank you for considering him," Estella exclaimed.

"Relax then witches," Damien commanded.

Raven, who had been channeling immense loads of power all night, dropped the spell, and the golden glow immediately faded.

Liam began to cry, as he had apparently found the energy comforting. Estella rushed to pick the baby up, fussing and cooing and putting him to her breast.

Raven slumped. She was sweating, and looked pale with dehydration and effort. Damien ordered the witch carried into one of the bedrooms, where Carlice plied her with fluids and sponged her forehead. Paul and John Booth had been working carefully within their capacity, but both were tired and ravenously hungry.

Lena Lenore led them to easy chairs in the lounge and offered to cook a meal. The Booth father and son put their feet up on cushions and looked immensely pleased. No one had pampered them since

Paul's mother had died many years ago.

Zarah Strahan rushed to Paul Booth's side and began cooing over him. The two juniors had been slowly negotiating the path from 'just good friends' to coupledom over the past few weeks and the stress of the previous night had proved to be a motivating factor. They shared a little kiss despite the presence of assorted school and community members.

Estella turned to Eduard Nevermore who was hovering in the lounge somewhat uncertainly while his girlfriend was busy cooking. "Could you drive us home please?" she requested. "I don't feel safe out there alone, and I need to check on my husband and mother-in-law."

"Of course," Eduard said. He led the way out of the side door of the manor to the private parking area. "Which car is yours Estella?"

"This one," Estella unlocked the car and slotted Liam's carrycot back into the baby seat, where it held him safe and secure during travel. She handed Eduard the keys. "You drive please. I feel shaky."

"It's been a long night," Eduard remarked. He accepted the keys and slid into the drivers' seat. Estella and Ivy took their seats and Eduard triggered the ignition. "Seat belts please."

The girls were too tired for talking during the short drive back to the Pinkerton house. Eduard parked the car in the driveway and returned the keys to Estella.

"I can walk home," he said. "I will be fine."

"That might not be necessary," Estella said pointing to Captain Etheridge's utility vehicle which was also parked in the driveway. "It looks as though the Captain is here."

Estella unlocked the front door and stepped inside. "Sunny, Grandmother - is everything okay?"

"My mother is lying down," Sunny replied hugging his wife warmly. "The night has been very stressful for her. However, I was glad to know you two were safe at the Manor." He turned to Eduard. "I owe you and your brother my thanks for looking after them."

"It was our pleasure," Eduard replied. "Estella was a great comfort to us at the manor too."

"Estella is like that," Sunny said, enveloping her with more hugs.

"Where is Captain Etheridge?" Ivy asked. "I see his car, but he isn't here."

"The Captain and the big dog chased a prowler from the farmland into the estates," Sunny said. "I wanted to go along and help them, but the Cap' said I had to protect mother."

"Quite right too," Eduard said. "If you don't mind, Mr. Pinkerton sir, I will wait until the Captain returns."

"You are welcome," Sunny said. "Please call me Sunny, I am a simple farmer and no one's sir."

"My family came to America to farm several generations ago," Eduard said. "You are carrying on the honorable tradition."

"Thank you for saying so," Sunny said.

"Your family, now I've been meaning to ask you about them sometime," Old Mrs. Pinkerton murmured, appearing from her section of the house with her hair slightly mussed. "Young Eduard Nevermore."

"You are awake mother," Sunny exclaimed.

"Yes, I heard our visitor arrive," Old Mrs. Pinkerton exclaimed. She surveyed Eduard critically. "Has anyone told you that you are the splitting image of Edvard Ermore? And your brother – so like Darrian Ermore."

"I have heard it said occassionally," Eduard admitted.

"I found a picture in some old photos we were going through to mark the sesquicentenary of our church," Mrs. Pinkerton continued. "The present building of course. There was an older building I think, but it was on a different spot."

"I believe the family name was Ermore once," Eduard said. "Then somewhere along the line, it split into Nevermore and Blackermore. It was so long ago that the current family members do not even bother to look into it."

"I wonder if Grandma Strahan remembers anything," Old Mrs. Pinkerton mused. "She used to go out with Edward Nevermore. I forget why she didn't marry him. That Edward would have been your grandfather wouldn't he?"

"Yeah," Eduard was growing pink. "The name has remained in the family."

Ivy laughed and gave Eduard a friendly poke. "No wonder Christy Strahan hates you!" she said. "Well I would love to see Jaylen, but I am tired, so I will be going to bed for a little nap. Enjoy gossiping with my grandmother."

"I need to go to bed too," Estella said. She handed Liam to

Sunny. "He is all fed. Someone who got some sleep please wake me for lunch."

Poor Eduard was left all alone in the kitchen with Grandmother Pinkerton, who was still trying to work out why Grandmother Strahan had decided not to marry Edward Nevermore when they were young. In the end she concluded that Grandfather Strahan must have promised to be much more reliable. Eduard listened politely, but staunchly refused to comment.

****

When Ivy woke later, Estella was sitting in the rocking chair nursing Liam. The day seemed unusually peaceful in comparison to the preceding night.

"There are pancakes in the warmer," Estella said.

"Thanks," Ivy said. She crossed into the kitchen and lifted the lid: "Mm."

"Normally you would be at school," Estella said.

"I will ask Mr. Yore for an extra credit essay," Ivy said.

"Better ask all your teachers," Estella advised. "Ivy, your father and I are worried that between funeral days, the Sheriff organizing hunting days, and other events, your senior year is being interrupted! First term is almost over and there have been a number of emergencies."

"It has been a bit disruptive," Ivy agreed.

"Have you thought about universities for next year?" Estella inquired.

"Oh I'm applying to Mercer, Georgia State University and even Mystic Evermore Community College," Ivy said. "I've never understood the urge to get into an institution outside of my home state. They all offer an education, even though some have higher reputations than others!"

"I wouldn't know anything about it," Estella said. "I'm from a different place altogether, and I don't know how long I have been alive, let alone how I was educated. I just know that your father would like the best for you."

There was a knock at the door. Jaylen stood there looking mildly comical in his Mystic Evermore High uniform after all the drama. "I wanted to see whether you were all right," he stammered.

"Young love," Estella said. "How sweet."

Jaylen blushed. "You aren't so very old yourself Mrs. Pinkerton," he returned. "Would you be ready for school soon Ivy, so I can give you a lift?"

"Sure," Ivy said. She swallowed down the last of her pancake and raced into her room to find her school skirt and blazer. Luckily they were not too creased and a fresh shirt made the outfit quite presentable.

"Goodbye Estella," she called and rushed out of the door.

Ivy jumped into the car and Jaylen started the engine immediately.

"Imagine being one of the 'normal' teens who have no idea the town was under attack last night," Jaylen chortled.

"Now I'm in the know, I can't conceive that," Ivy remarked to Jaylen. "But Estella was asking me about next year - what do you think you will be doing?"

"Ah the dreaded future talk," Jaylen said. He reached down and took Ivy's hand even though he was driving. The other hand remained steady on the steering wheel. "My mother isn't going to like this, but I'm planning to learn a trade. The Woodgates built this city once, and I don't see why I shouldn't get back to doing so literally."

Ivy giggled. "Tradies have an odd sort of power," she said. "Power and control over those who can't make or do anything themselves."

"Exactly," Jaylen agreed. "Although I don't think my mother, the Mayor, will see it that way!"

"Are you sure though?" Ivy asked. "You could have a football scholarship to any university you wanted."

"Yeah, I'm sure," Jaylen said. "What about you?"

"I thought I would study Nursing," Ivy said. "Ever since Melissa and Christy got hurt, I've wanted to help people."

"That sounds great," Jaylen said. "But don't forget, we have the rest of this year to enjoy. Our senior year should be fun!"

"Of course," Ivy agreed. They drove into the school yard and Jaylen selected a parking space for the vehicle. "See you in class."

The remaining hours of the school day flew quickly. Ivy looked around for Christy, but the vampire girl was not in attendance that day, probably sleeping off the romantic night she had with Wilson the previous evening.

Then Jaylen had football practice, and he invited Ivy to watch the football training, before going out for milkshakes with Fenton and Carlice. Jaylen hesitated when he asked this, because Ivy had not wanted to spend time with Carlice when he had suggested a road trip together, but Ivy had grown in confidence during the past days. She replied that she would be perfectly comfortable, if Carlice was accompanied by her new boyfriend.

When football practice concluded, Jaylen stopped by the bench where Ivy was sitting and sat down beside her panting. He was fatigued today, and the exercise had even raised a slight perspiration across his temple. Ivy thought he looked very cute, hot and puppy-like.

"My poor Jay," Ivy said, massaging his shoulders and neck briefly. "Running around all day and all night."

"That's nothing," Jaylen said. "After a drink and a snack, I will have plenty of energy again. But I better hit the changing rooms for a quick shower before we go." He gave Ivy a brief. but sweet peck on the lips. "I won't be a minute."

Jaylen was considerably more than a minute in the showers of course, and Ivy amused herself by watching the butterflies playing amongst the flowers. So amazing to remember the beautiful creatures were caterpillars a few short days ago, and had recently crawled out of cocoons.

The butterflies reminded her of the capsule in her stepmothers' spacecraft. Had Estella been hatched from that capsule in her human form, leaving a previous alien form behind? Perhaps they would never know. All that was known was that Estella was as bright and beautiful as a butterfly today.

Jaylen returned, interrupting Ivy's thoughts. They jumped into the four wheel drive and drove to the Snack Bar, which the most popular of the after school dining spots. Fenton Etheridge and Carlice Favor were already sitting in a booth sipping their milk shakes. Carlice apparently liked a strong looking strawberry flavour, while Fenton enjoyed vanilla.

"Everybody seems to be here tonight," Ivy murmured. "Even kids who weren't at school today."

Ivy nodded towards Paul Booth, who was sitting at a large table with Zarah Strahan, along with his older brother Wilson and Christy Strahan. Benji Strahan was next to them, talking earnestly to Jeroma Tilton and Netta Davis. Several members of the party smiled and nodded back.

Raven Booth was settled into a private corner booth along with her best friend Lena Lenore, and clandestine squeeze Jamie Lenore. Neither girl acknowledged Ivy, but Jamie gave her a slight wink.

Mike Davis and Javier Tilton were at a table which was loaded with hamburgers and onion rings, two hungry boys out for an evening snack without any female company.

"Your regular is chocolate isn't it?" Jaylen asked.

"I think I'll have malt tonight," Ivy said, her taste buds craving the mellow sweetness.

"Hey there," Carlice said, waving. "We saved you seats."

"Hey there," Ivy echoed, slipping into the booth opposite Carlice and Fenton while Jaylen went to make their order.

"It's wonderful that Jaylen has found someone who understands him," Carlice said. "You do don't you Ivy?"

"I certainly do," Ivy said, although she privately believed she did not need to be answering personal questions from Jaylen's ex-girlfriend.

"I haven't seen Jaylen so happy since I have known him," Fenton observed. "Which I admit has only been a few months, but it's great to see you two together."

"It's great to see you two together too," Ivy said.

"I needed a little lone time after my mother died," Fenton said, "And while I will never be over her death - at least I can grieve in company now. Carlice is a great support."

Ivy nodded empathetically.

Fenton cleared his throat. "I say, I hope you don't mind, but Damien Nevermore didn't drop by the school to collect Didge like he often does, so we had to bring her with us. I know it was meant to be just us four."

"That's alright," Ivy murmured, although it wasn't really alright with her. Rumor had it, Jaylen had a crush on Bridget Etheridge when she had first arrived in town. Moreover, the cubicles were perfect for four and squishy with five.

Jaylen returned with their shakes and slid into the cubicle alongside Ivy. "You would never guess who I ran into at the check-out," he said to Fenton. "Your sister!"

"I couldn't leave her out man," Fenton protested.

"That's quite all right," Jaylen said. "I'm always happy to see Didge." Jaylen slid out of the bench again and swiped a dining chair from one of the regular tables, attentively placing it at the edge of the booth for Bridget. Now when she sat down, the red-haired girl could view both couples comfortably.

"Thanks Jaylen," Bridget said brightly. She sat on the chair and sipped at her milk shake. Ivy noticed it was lime, her own least favorite.

Javier Tilton had apparently also noticed that Bridget was unaccompanied as he came over to their table to try and make an impression. "Hello," he said. "Are you alone tonight Bridget?"

Bridget was unenthused. "Yes, Javier," she said. "Please don't make a big deal of it. I'm not in the mood tonight."

"Another time perhaps buddy," Jaylen said protectively, and Javier went back to the table he had been sharing with Mike.

Ivy privately wished that Bridget had accepted Javier's invitation, instead of continuing to intrude on her date with Jaylen.

"So what's new?" Ivy asked, in an attempt to change the subject.

"Someone said Miss Byall went on a date with Mr. Yore," Fenton said. "But it might not be true, the teachers go places together all the time."

"I thought Miss Byall was looking at your dad," Ivy said tartly.

"That better not be true," Bridget said. "Dad is so not ready to date again! Miss Byall would just get hurt."

"Teachers and parents dating is just gross," Carlice said. "And probably against the law - I must ask my mother, she would know!"

"So who was the big guy from last night?" Ivy inquired. "Any ideas?"

Carlice pulled a couple of dollar notes out of her pocket and laid them on the table. "Well, I'm not sure," she said, thumbing the twenty. "But maybe..."

"Really?" Fenton exclaimed. "It couldn't be."

"Looks a bit like," Jaylen said. "Given that is not a very good portrait."

"It doesn't really matter, does it - so long as he stays up in Tennessee and keeps his word to Damien?" Bridget remarked.

"That is the main point," Fenton said.

"I feel weird," Jaylen said. "I'm the only one who didn't get to see this fellow."

"You were doing your job," Ivy said, patting his knee. "And you were very good at it."

"I could do with some fries," Carlice announced, and Fenton climbed out past Bridget to collect a new food order for the group. The teenagers ate and chatted for half-an-hour or so longer, then they said their farewells and agreed to go their separate ways.

Ivy was glad they were leaving. While Carlice had been no threat, Jaylen had been more chivalrous towards Bridget than she had expected. Now Ivy was worried that he was not really over the red-headed Etheridge twin.

After all a crush was hard to extinguish, and unrequited love never got to run its true course. The object of such affection frequently remained on a pedestal for some time. Ivy trusted Jaylen implicitly, but she was still aware their relationship was new.

It was getting dark when the students entered the car park. The moon was low in the sky and the first stars were beginning to twinkle. Ivy and Jaylen were on their way to the four wheel drive, when she heard a rustle in the large charity bin parked behind the store. Normally rustles in bins meant small rodents, but in Mystic Evermore, strange noises could mean anything.

"Do you think we had better check that out?" Ivy whispered to Jaylen.

Jaylen crossed to the charity bin and lifted the flap. A figure was crouched inside, shielding its eyes from the last remnants of daylight.

"What do we have here?" Jaylen exclaimed.

Carlice also crossed the car park in less than seconds. She clamped a surprisingly strong hand around the figure's wrist and hauled him out of the charity bin.

"A rogue vampire," she announced. "Snuck into town after the protection circle was dropped last night."

"What shall we do with him?" Jaylen asked. "Captain Etheridge's rules would say capture, not kill, now the war is over."

"Why he does not look so very different than us," Bridget

exclaimed and Fenton nodded.

"It's true," the Vampire said. "I was only nineteen when I was changed."

"Do you have a name?" Ivy asked curiously.

"Yes, it is Christopher," the vampire said. "And if you please, I'm not a rogue."

"You are one of the vampires that attacked us last night," Carlice insisted firmly.

"General Jackson is a hard man to resist," Christopher said. "I have a peaceful heart really, but I had to obey."

Fenton nodded. "I once read that Jackson announced any man who refused to fight for him would be shot," he said.

Christopher gave him a puzzled look. "That sort of thing, although I don't know where you would have read about it."

"Well you have to go and see Damien Nevermore immediately!" Carlice declared. "Jaylen please drive us - I can't risk letting Christopher go."

"Do you need me to come along?" Fenton offered.

"Follow in the other car with Ivy and Bridget in case there is trouble," Carlice suggested. "Once again, I can't place any of you humans in close proximity to Christopher."

Ivy, Fenton and Bridget climbed into the Etheridge's car and were hardly underway, when Bridget tapped her brother on the shoulder.

"Could you please drop me off at home along the way?" Bridget asked. "I didn't feel like seeing Damien toady."

"You don't feel like seeing Damien Nevermore?" Fenton teased. "Well that is a new one!"

Bridget flushed. "We have been broken up for some time now," she said. "I just realized we need to start acting like it."

"Dad and I agree with you on that one," Fenton said. "But I'm afraid I can't stop now, our house is a bit out of the way and Jaylen is driving quite fast."

"So drive faster," Bridget objected. "The Sheriff won't book you."

"The Sheriff probably won't book Jaylen, because he is on an emergency mission," Fenton said. "I'm not so sure about us. You will just have to face up to Damien, Didge. You have no problem when you want to."

"Alright," Bridget subsided glumly.

Ivy now felt sorry for Bridget. She could recall how she felt when Mike Davis forgot they had played together as children and began to chase all the other girls in the class. Damien's protectiveness toward Sheriff Favor the previous evening must have felt similar for Bridget. Not that Ivy was willing to give Bridget her boyfriend as a consolation prize.

The two vehicles twisted through the suburbs, finally arriving at Nevermore Manor. Jaylen got out and opened the rear door for Carlice and her prisoner. Carlice climbed out, dragging Christopher after her.

"Is Damien home?" Carlice cried, as Eduard answered the summons of the manor house door bell.

"You are in luck," Eduard said. "He was just about to go out hunting rogue vampires, but he hasn't left yet."

"We found a straggler," Jaylen explained.

Eduard inspected Christopher closely. "He almost smells almost honest," Eduard said. "What do you think Jaylen?"

"I thought it worth bringing him here," Jaylen said.
"He said he is not a killer, but he could be a spy," Carlice added. "He admits to being from Tennessee."

"Hmm," Eduard said. "All that is for Damien to determine."

"What is for Damien to determine?" Damien Nevermore inquired, appearing behind his brother. "Ah a prisoner. Put him in the cellar and lock the door until I can interview him properly."

"Don't worry," Eduard said to the frightened looking Christopher. "Our cellar is probably a lot nicer than wherever you spent the day." He disappeared into the house with Christopher securely held by the arm. "You might even get a bottle of lambs' blood if you are lucky."

"Something would be appreciated," Christopher was heard to say as they left. "It gets far harder to resist biting humans when you are hungry."

"Bridget my dear," Damien said, noticing the occupants of the second car for the first time. "Why won't you greet me?"

"I'm sorry Damien," Bridget said. "I think you know why."

"I have never lied to you Bridget," Damien said. "Well maybe a little at first." He reached through the car window and traced his index finger down the veins in her throat, almost to the vulnerable curve of her cleavage.

Bridget shivered and her chest heaved. "Don't Damien," she whispered.

Damien withdrew his hand: "Sheriff Favor seems more willing to accept me for who I am, than she was once," he admitted. "There is nothing going on between us, at the moment... but maybe I would like there to be one day. If I ever come to deserve a chance with a human woman... I'm still not sure about that!"

"Don't embarrass Bridget in front of her brother and friends," Ivy spoke up bravely.

Damien spared her a fleeting glance. "Ah - little church girl, Ivy Pinkerton," he said. "How is Estella today?"

"She is well, thank you for asking," Ivy's tone was slightly sarcastic.

"Her contribution was much appreciated," Damien said. "Never think of me as ungrateful. Now I have to be off and act as the big bad of north Georgia."

"Do you want my help?" Jaylen asked.

"Take the night off and get some sleep," Damien said. He checked his belt for his sword and a bundle of stakes. "So long guys. Stay safe if you can." He turned and strode away into the blackening night without bothering to take his car.

"Damien was a bit rude don't you think?" Fenton complained. "After the way everybody supported him last night and all."

"He is under a lot of stress," said Eduard, who had returned from locking Christopher in the cellar. "Would you guys like to come inside?"

"I think we should be going after all," Jaylen said. "Ivy please come back into my car?"

Ivy climbed into Jaylen's all-wheel-drive beside him, and Carlice rejoined Fenton in his car. Now everyone was with their right partner, except for Bridget, who had yet to find her human soulmate. Or if she had already met a suitable candidate, open her heart and let him into her life.

"Are you sure you don't want Bridget?" Ivy whispered. "She seems to be free now."

"There are plenty of other boys in the class who might fancy Bridget," Jaylen said. "Including Javier Tilton, if she ever stops viewing him as a vampire wannabe and gets to know him for himself."

"But that would be another story wouldn't it?" Ivy whispered.

"Yeah," Jaylen agreed. "This particular chapter was our very own special love story."

Jaylen drove Bridget towards her home, but he stopped the car a few meters before he got to the Pinkerton house. They were under a bushy tree, whose shade was not required at night, but was handy for privacy. It wasn't quite Lovers' Lane but it would do.

"Engine trouble?" Ivy joked.

"I haven't given you a proper kiss," Jaylen whispered.

Ivy traced her hands across Jaylen's chest, around his neck and out over his shoulders. Then she returned her hands to his rib cage. "Your heart beats so hard."

"It beats for you," Jaylen whispered.

"Your skin is so hot," Ivy whispered. "Anyone would think you had a fever."

"That is normal for me," Jaylen said. "So the only fever I have is love."

Ivy raised her mouth for his kiss. "I love you too Jaylen," she whispered.

The heat of his wolverine body set her on fire even though a cool breeze had sprung up and was wafting through a gap between the window glass and doorframe. As first pashes went, this one was proving to be pretty good.

"Tell me if I am moving too fast," Jaylen whispered as his hands gathered her to him and traced the outline of her back.

"A little," Ivy whispered, "But it feels good!" She began to giggle. "Estella - my stepmother, said we would have puppies."

"That's a new one!" Jaylen muttered into her cheek as he kissed the line between her ear and her mouth before returning to her mouth. "We will see whether we can turn the Woodgate curse into a blessing."

"I certainly hope that we can," Ivy whispered. She stopped Jaylen's hand as it fumbled with her back-strap. "Leave something for another day."

"I had better walk you to the door then," Jaylen said. "I'm only a footy player, and I'm not given to poetic fancy - but we will have many other days I hope.... That's my clumsy way of asking you to go steady."

"Yes and yes!" Ivy said. "I'm glad we got that clear!"

Jaylen started the car again and drove Ivy the few meters to the Pinkerton house. He engaged the handbrake and walked around the car to help Ivy out. Then he activated the central locking and led her the few steps to her front porch. They shared one more very sweet kiss and then Ivy used her key to unlock the front door. Ivy slipped inside and passed the lounge room door.

Estella was sitting in her regular chair nursing Liam, and Sunny was sitting opposite reading the *Farmer's Monthly* newsletter. The couple were the perfect picture of happiness and tranquility. Estella was beginning to glow just slightly around the edges, and Liam was also emitting a soft aura. Ivy understood how they felt and wished as much happiness for everyone else in Mystic Evermore and the whole wide world.

****

ABOUT THE AUTHOR

Cecelia is an Australian author and poet who has a special interest in American Literature. In 1993 she completed a Master's thesis on H.P. Lovecraft and the 'Gothic' or 'weird tale'. She followed this with a study of the Fairy Tale Motif in Victorian Literature in 1996, also at Masters' level.

Today, Cecelia is hard at work creating her own fairy tales and myths.

Cecelia is also the author of:

Special Pictures to Talk About (ISBN: 978-0-646-97235-0), which developed out of her work on language delay and speech development in Kindergartens.

Silver Springtime (ISBN-13: 978-0-6481160-1-1), the first of a series of period romances following the developmental struggles of a group of teenagers attending a Christian university in the 1980s.

All for Love (ISBN: 978-0-6481160-2-8), the first of a reality television spin-off romance series.

Mystic Evermore (ISBN: 978-0-6481160-0-4), the first of the vampire series "Nevermore Parables".

Faith and Love (ISBN: 978-0-6481160-3-5) - the second of a series of Christian university romances.